INTO YOU

AMITY MALCOM

COPYRIGHT

DEDICATION

To anyone who has ever felt unworthy of love because of who they are.

AUTHOR'S NOTE

While a work of fiction, Sew Into You touches on many realities that face the LGBTQIA+ community on a daily basis. Throughout the story, you will find themes of religious trauma as well as familial abandonment.

Please always consider your mental health when starting any book.

The Luna Sea Plaza series takes place in a fictional not-so-distant future where cannabis has been legalized for recreational use. If you disagree with cannabis use for medical or recreational use, this is not the series for you.

Prologue
Imogen

THE FIRST TIME I FELL IN LOVE, I WAS SEVEN YEARS OLD.

Of course, that doesn't mean that I lived a life without love until that point. I loved and was loved by my parents, my cousins, and especially by my grandma, Birdie. But it was that familiar love that came with those related to me, the type of love that I held for family and friends. Not the type of love that was saved for fairy tales and happily-ever-afters, the bone-crushing love that I simply could not live without.

Sitting at a small, wooden desk in my second-grade classroom, I was focused on the math worksheet I was working on, unaware that the door to the classroom had opened. Head down, number two pencil clutched firmly in my tiny grasp, it wasn't until my teacher spoke that I lifted my head and pushed my long, brown hair away from my face.

Next to my teacher, at the front of the classroom, a tiny girl stood with tentative shyness.

She looked like a darling little cherub, the kind normally seen in old artwork of little angels flitting behind bold, curvy, Renaissance women.

Large, brown eyes looked back into the sea of faces that were focused on the newcomer. Blonde hair the color of straw cascaded around a heart-shaped face in bouncy curls, while a single rhinestone-studded bow held the strands from falling into her face. I didn't know why, but I was jealous of that bow. Not jealous that she had one and I didn't but was jealous of the bow itself as it carefully held her hair in place.

Her lips were so pink that I imagined she had just finished a strawberry lollipop before entering the classroom, and when she gave a small smile as our teacher introduced her to the class, I noticed little dimples that appeared on either side of her lips.

She made my insides feel warm and fuzzy, like a gooey brownie fresh from the oven on a cold, rainy day.

"Boys and girls, I want to introduce you to Esme," our teacher said. "Her family just moved here from Nebraska, and she'll be joining our class. I expect you all to be kind to our new friend and to give her the warmest Wildcat welcome you can."

Together, teacher and student, walked to her desk, where she pulled out a small chair for Esme to sit. While everyone around us had gone back to their work, I couldn't take my eyes off the little girl that sat timidly at the front of the classroom, only bowing my head to return to my work when our teacher stood up from behind her chair.

"Imogen," my teacher's voice was soft when she spoke, "if it is okay with you, I would like to have Esme share a desk with you for the rest of the day. Would it be okay if she sat with you and followed along while we do the rest of our work?"

Only too eager to accept her offer, I nodded, scooting my chair over so Esme could sit next to me on her own hard, plastic chair where we spent the remainder of the afternoon following along with the rest of the students in our class.

I snuck careful glances her way throughout the rest of the day, enamored by her small quirks—like the way the very tip of her tongue poked out while she was deep in concentration working on something, or the way she scrunched up her nose as if pushing an imaginary pair of glasses up the bridge.

We whispered with our heads closely tucked together as I helped to explain our work, one of her curls brushing against my cheek. I wanted to reach out and touch that curl, to lightly pull it and watch it spring back into place, to see if it felt as soft against my fingers as it did against my face.

But I stopped myself, not wanting to come across as some weird girl that she didn't want to sit next to. For some reason that was unknown to me at the time, I was terrified of Esme not wanting to be close to me the way I wanted to be close to her.

Against all odds, by the end of that first day, Esme and I cemented ourselves as new best friends. Finding out that her parents were the people who bought the house only a few doors down from my own only made my heart patter faster, and I was already excited at the prospect of future sleepovers and late-night giggles.

It wasn't long before I quickly lost count of the number of those sleepovers we had, spending nights watching movies, binge-eating popcorn and pizza, and giving each other horrendous makeovers with the few little makeup kits I owned.

Over our first summer together, Grandma Birdie helped us each to make our own quilt so that we could have matching blankets during our sleepovers. A master at sewing, my grandmother made everything from doll clothes and purses, to placemats and pillows. But where she really shined was in the gorgeous quilts she painstakingly worked on for hours at a time.

Grandma Birdie took us to the local crafting store, helping us to pick out bright fabrics in pinks, yellows, and oranges, all the while complaining that our town really needed a proper quilt store. She guided us in cutting the fabric into the appropriately sized pieces for the intricate pattern we chose, in laying out each piece where it belonged before sewing, and stood by, a willing helpful hand, while both Esme and myself learned how to operate one of her three sewing machines.

The quilts were thick and warm, and despite the summer heat, when they were finished—quilted with a grandmother's careful and meticulous love—we spent every spare moment under those quilts while we giggled well past our bedtimes.

We were under those quilts when we were ten years old, Esme confessing that she had a crush on a boy in her class but that she was nervous because she overheard one of his friends saying that he wanted to kiss her. Pink tinged her cheeks, and I wasn't sure if it was embarrassment or something else that caused the blush to spread across her face. Esme's blush was as beautiful as the rest of her, and I found myself forcing my eyes away from her face at the strange feeling that was bubbling up inside my own chest.

"I've never done that before. Kissed a boy, I mean. What If I'm horrible at it and he doesn't like me after it?" she confessed.

I hadn't kissed a boy either. But honestly, the idea of it kind of grossed me out.

No, I didn't want to kiss a boy.

Sometimes, though, I thought about kissing Esme. About her perfectly pink lips, the color of an unused eraser that one might be gifted on the first day of school. The one that someone would be determined to keep as pristine as possible, trying their hardest not to make a mistake for fear of having to mar its perfect color with ugly, black smudges. I thought about how full her lips were and how soft they would feel pressed against my own, like tiny pillows that cradled my head and neck at night in just the right way when I crawled into bed after an exhaustingly long day.

"Why don't you just practice?" I asked, still afraid to look back into her mesmerizing eyes.

Esme laughed, a giggle that shook the bed we shared. "How do you suppose I practice? On my hand? On a pillow filled with gross feathers?"

My mouth opened before my brain could register what I was about to say. "You could practice with me."

I immediately regretted the words as fear slicked across my body. The small hairs pricked to life on the back of my neck while I simultaneously tried to chase away the tendrils of panic that raced up my spine. Afraid she was going to run away from me, that she was going to laugh, or worse yet, tell someone what I had just said, I tried to backtrack, but the look on her face stopped me.

Her eyes were wide, irises the same color of warm honey as she searched my face. "You would do that for me?"

Smiling back at her as some of the panic dissipated, I didn't hesitate before telling her the truth. "I'd do anything for you, Es."

Slowly, we inched closer together, fumbling as we lightly pressed our lips against one another. It was chaste and quick, a mere peck that lasted for seconds.

But I wanted it to last forever.

"See, that wasn't so bad," I told her after as I stared ahead, fairly certain the smile on my face would never fade.

We returned to whatever movie was playing, my fingers lightly tracing my lips where Esme's had been just seconds before. And while I wanted to ask her what she thought, if she would ever want to kiss me again, we didn't speak about it for a few years until she was over for another Friday night sleepover when we were fifteen.

Her head was against my shoulder as we sat in my bed together. It was a common enough occurrence, the two of us cuddled against one another as we sat under the same quilts we had been using for years. I never found it to be odd. More than anything, I was comforted by her touch and honored that she felt safe enough to lean on me—both literally and figuratively.

We had been sitting in comfortable silence for a few minutes before she spoke on a long exhale. "Immy, do you remember the time we kissed?"

I looked down at my beautiful angel with questioning eyes, almost amused at the thought that I could ever forget that kiss.

That's how I saw Esme every time I looked at her. As my own personal angel brought into my life to surround me with happiness and light. The years hadn't lessened the feelings I had for the sandy-haired beauty. Instead, they only strengthened them. And while she had slowly begun to show interest in boys, my interest was only ever on her.

I held steadfast over the fact that we would always be friends and that I would be content to watch Esme from the sidelines, always loving her from afar. I never planned to tell her how deeply I longed to be closer to her, how I yearned to love her as more than a friend, and how I coveted her the way most girls my age felt about the popular boys in our grade. While I knew there were women in the world who loved other women and men who loved other men, I didn't think that it was the same for me. I simply loved Esme and longed to be close to her in whatever small way I could, even if I knew that meant we were destined to always be simply friends.

"Of course I do," I told her honestly. "We were under the same quilts we are now, and you were so worried you would mess something up. I didn't like seeing you unsure of yourself, so I offered to practice with you."

She closed her eyes, shutting them tightly as if she was trying to ward off a bad memory as she shook her head back and forth. Her curls bounced around her face in my favorite chaotic way, making her look like a little woodland sprite. "I think something is wrong with me."

Concerned, I pushed myself up straight, my back against the headboard so I could fully look at my friend's face. Still, she didn't open her eyes to look at me. Instead, she started to speak again, her voice barely above a whisper. "Marley Stetson kissed me at lunch today."

My insides started to tumble, and my cheeks heated in a mixture of anger and jealousy. I wanted to be happy for her, but I couldn't find it in myself to school my features into anything but a grimace.

"He followed me when I went out to the bathroom, and before I knew what was happening, he had me against the brick wall outside the girl's room and his tongue was in my mouth. For some reason, I let him kiss me. I didn't stop him, didn't kiss him back, but the entire time he was kissing me, I just kept thinking about how gross it was. About how gross *he* was."

Objectively speaking, Marley Stetson was the best-looking boy in school.

If I were into that type of thing.

I certainly didn't think I would ever be into Marley Stetson—or any other boy for that matter.

Esme continued, eyes still closed, "Any girl in our class would have been thrilled to be in my position, and yet I felt nothing but disgust. Every time a boy kisses me or tries to touch me, it's all I feel, Immy. Like it's wrong, like I'm not supposed to have their lips on mine."

I reached out and linked my fingers through hers, simply wanting to comfort her but selfishly loving the way her hand fit in mine. "Why do you think that means something is wrong with you?"

She let out a shuddering breath, like it physically hurt her to speak. It broke my heart into a million pieces to see her so unsure of herself, and I wanted to do something...*anything*...to take her pain away.

Finally opening her eyes, she looked at me, her gaze as uneasy and pained as the rest of her delicate facial features. "Because, Immy, every time some boy kisses me, I think back to that night when we first kissed, and I think about how badly I want it to be *you* again."

For maybe the first time in my life, I was speechless.

Esme, my angel, the very girl I fell in love with the second I saw her...

She wanted to kiss me again?

The moment her words finally registered in my head, I sprang to action, pulling her closer to me. I studied her face closely, searching her eyes and trying to convey words without speaking. Gently tucking a stray lock of hair behind her ear, I leaned in closer, pressing my lips to hers.

Esme stiffened for a second and just as I was starting to second-guess myself, she melted into the kiss, pressing back against my lips with hers. Those same lips that I knew years later were not stained by any sweet treat, that no artificial color could ever match the exact color pink of her full lips. I gently parted my lips, licking across the seam of her mouth, surprised when she allowed me to enter. We were messy and inexperienced as we explored each other, two young girls sharing an experience for the first time.

I never wanted it to end.

For six glorious months, Esme and I were even more inseparable than we had already been. We shared secret kisses in the hallway at school, stealing a few moments between classes whenever we could. We sat in the back row at the movie theater, fingers threaded between one another's as we fed each other Twizzlers and shared oversized sodas. We talked and laughed, shared plans for the future…for *our* future.

Like clockwork, we alternated between houses on the weekends, sharing kisses under the covers during our almost-weekly sleepovers. We giggled together as we ran our hands over each other's bodies in unskilled motions; we gasped together as we explored the most sacred places and learned about the pleasure we could bring one another, and we confessed our love to one another as we watched the sun rise together on the morning of my sixteenth birthday.

She was my everything, my one and only, the girl I was going to spend the rest of my life with.

Until she was gone.

The first time I had my heart broken, I was sixteen years old.

One
Imogen

"WHAT THE FUCK?"

A huge pop sounds from somewhere in the parking lot of the shopping plaza before our entire quilt shop falls into near black. While only a little after seven in the evening, the late February sun is already fading quickly, and it will be only minutes until we are completely shrouded in a combination of darkness and shadows.

From somewhere toward the back of the shop, Grandma Birdie appears, a small flashlight in hand. "What the fuck is right, dear. Any idea what's going on?"

While Grandma Birdie is in her seventies, she is still one of the most colorful people I have ever met—in both her language and her personality. Today, she wears a maxi dress sewn together with dark floral fabrics that is undoubtedly a creation of her own. A faux fur vest is unzipped over top of the dress, and several chunky, beaded necklaces hang loosely around her neck.

Growing up, I always knew my grandmother was different from most others. While my friends had grandparents that did things like take their grandchildren out to dinner or maybe to a movie, I had a grandmother that took me to see *The Grateful Dead* cover bands and accidentally served pot-laced brownies to my friends at my college graduation party.

Although, if I'm being completely honest, I'm not sure how much of an accident those brownies were.

Grandma Birdie—real name Roberta—is as much of a hippie

as they come. When she was twenty-three, she attended the original Woodstock, still lives every ounce of the *make love, not war* motto the community is often known for, and to this day, she rocks flowing hair that cascades down to the middle of her back. Only now, it's a brilliant silver as opposed to the rich, dark brown of her younger days.

I've always been told that I'm the spitting image of her as a younger woman, and I'll forever take it as a compliment. We share the same sharp facial features and Roman noses, the same deep green eyes, and curvy body type. Not so many years ago, we also shared our height, but as she has aged, she has lost a few inches, which she will deny until she takes her last breath.

As my grandmother reaches my side with her flashlight, I pull my phone from my back pocket, using the built-in flashlight app to further illuminate our space. Together, we exit the shop, looking at the now-dark sign adorned with the name of our shop —The Grateful Thread.

See? Total hippie.

One quick glance shows us that it's not only our shop that is dark. Every store that makes up Luna Sea Plaza looks like it has been left deserted. For a shopping plaza usually illuminated under various neon signs and lamp posts, the sight is almost eerie and foreboding.

I can just about make out Maeve at the end of the strip mall, standing out front of her bookstore—Black, White, and Read All Over. Asher stands with Hollis outside of Frisky Business, the adult toy store that's connected to the quilt shop, and he gives us a shrug before pulling out his phone, typing away at the screen.

A breeze bustles across the parking lot, sending an unnerving shiver down my spine.

Leaning into me, Grandma Birdie breaks the silence. "Seems like the winds of change are coming."

I give her a little laugh. "Did your tarot cards tell you that, you crazy old lady?"

She harrumphs, giving me a gentle pat with the back of her hand. "Oh, you hush up, child. You know I'm just always a step or two ahead of the universe. Have been my entire life."

I comply in shutting my mouth, not because of her chastising, but because Grandma Birdie really does seem to have some sixth sense when it comes to predicting the future, and I don't think for a minute that her many decks of tarot cards have anything to do with it. If the woman ever wanted to get into gambling, there is no doubt in my mind that she could make an absolute killing when it came to sports betting.

I'm about to ask my grandmother if I should call the power company to report an outage when suddenly, the entire plaza lights back up. Across the parking lot, street lights flicker on while recessed lighting in the walkway in front of the buildings glows dimly overhead. One by one, the name of each shop in the plaza lights up.

Luna Sea Plaza is a mishmash of oddly unique businesses that all seem to mostly run well together. And while not intended, the play on the word *lunacy* that makes up the title of the shopping center is strangely accurate. Owned by one of Grandma Birdie's friends and fellow shop owner Watson, he gives us a hell of a discount on the rent for the shop. Although, I honestly think the discount is actually because the man has the hots for my grandma. Another fact she seems determined to ignore until her last breath.

Along with The Grateful Thread, the quilt shop I co-own with my grandmother, there is a bookstore, locksmith, adult toy store, metaphysical shop, convenience store, and an old-fashioned toy store.

See? True and utter lunacy.

As the last of the signs light up, my eyes are drawn to the left of the building where one lone shop has been sitting vacant for months. The previous tenants ran a successful jewelry shop from the location for nearly twenty years before deciding to retire to

Italy. Since they left, the place where the name of their store once sat illuminated has been an ugly rectangle of white light simply waiting to be filled with a beautiful, new sign.

Secretly, I have been hoping that whoever the new tenant ends up being, they are as progressive, inclusive, and inviting as the rest of us are. Well, all of us except the mysterious owner of the toy store, who was none too pleased to share space with an adult toy shop when Frisky Business opened up about two years ago.

My eyes go wide when they land on the sign where the plain white rectangle of light has been taunting me with its ugliness for the last few months. Instead, in a beautiful, green script, the words *High Tide* sit perfectly centered with tiny leaves around them. In smaller lettering under the name of the shop, the sign reads *Cannabis With Care.*

Grandma Birdie whoops enthusiastically next to me when she spots the illuminated sign. "Well, that's just something else! I tell you, if we had a full bath in the shop, I'd never have to leave the plaza! We've got the three most important words that start with S right here! Snacks, sex toys, and now, a smoke shop."

I try to ignore the fact that my grandmother all but just admitted to having a use for the sex toy shop next door, but try as I might, that's a sight I'm not sure I'll ever be able to banish from my mind.

Looking at me pointedly, she continues, "See? A new store moving into the plaza. Winds of change, Immy. Winds of change."

I smile at the use of my childhood nickname. There have only ever been two people in my life who called me Immy: my grandmother and the girl that stole my heart.

Esme.

Even now, nearly ten years since she disappeared from my life without a trace, thinking of her name causes tiny pieces of my heart to shatter. Part of me thinks it'll be that way for the rest of my life. That memories of her will sneak up on me at the most unexpected times. Sure, over time, the heartbreak has lessened, but it is still there in the dark recesses of my soul, and it's always just waiting to come out to play.

For tonight though, I push the bubbling thoughts back into those caverns within my soul, screwing the lid on tight.

Grandma Birdie and I return to the shop, quickly finishing up our closing tasks. While she sits behind the register, counting the till and doing paperwork, I walk the shop, making sure all of our brightly-colored fabric is in its proper place before running the vacuum over the worn, carpeted floors. While she used to protest, insisting to do the vacuuming and nightly cleaning, my grandmother has been slowing down as of late and finally gave in to swapping our nightly tasks when we close the shop together.

Upon finishing, I replace the vacuum before resting a hip against the hard corner of the check-out desk. I glance up at the kitchy signs that hang above the register and smile at my favorite: *may your bobbin always be full.*

"How old do I have to be for you to teach me your tricks?" I ask, reaching out to straighten another sign that reads, *I'm sew into you,* next to a cartoon drawing of a button and needle threaded with pink thread.

Looking up from under readers that are carefully perched on the bridge of her nose, my grandmother stares at me in confusion. "Teach you my tricks? And what are these tricks you speak of?"

"How the hell do you always know what's going to happen right before it does? You've been able to do it for as long as I can remember."

A gentle smile touches her lips as she lowers her readers and focuses her attention on me. "Sometimes, my sweet Imogen, when I was a young girl, I would get these feelings deep inside my belly. You know when you're someplace where the weather is cold outside and the heat is on high? The type of place where you pull a wool hat off your head and you can just feel the static course through your entire body? You know you need to touch something, but you're afraid of that small shock you simply know is going to occur. It feels something like that deep within my soul."

Hanging on her every word, I nod eagerly while she continues, a far-off look in her eyes. "I listened to those feelings every time I got one. I learned to trust that whatever static was inside me was showing me that something was about to happen. And for me, it always signified that while whatever was about to happen would be scary, that it would be absolutely worth it in the end."

My grandmother is the single most amazing person on this earth, and in this moment, I truly believe that she does have a connection to some higher being. I almost sigh out my next words. "So, that's how you knew that a new shop was going to be opening soon?"

She pointedly holds my stare for several seconds before bursting out into a cackling laugh, a full of life laugh that shakes her body. "No, you loon! I saw the guys from the sign company here this morning before you came in. I was just fucking with you out there!"

I stare back at her in wide-eyed disbelief, speechless that she would play me with such a dirty joke. "If there is a Hell, that's where you're headed, you evil woman."

She stands from the chair and retrieves her colorful, crocheted purse from beneath the desk. "It'll certainly be more entertaining than the alternative. Besides, I hate the cold. That's why I live in Florida. Bring on the flames, sweet child."

In comfortable silence, we lock up the shop and head to our cars. I make sure Birdie's car starts before settling behind the wheel of my own vehicle. With the key in the ignition, I'm about to start the engine when I take one last look toward our newest neighbor in the shopping plaza.

The inside of the building is dark, only slightly illuminated by the outside lights that shine into the space. In one corner, I can make out a few stacks of boxes, piled almost to the ceiling. Sweeping my gaze across the space, I'm momentarily frozen when I almost seem to lock eyes with a person on the other side of the glass.

In the dim light, I can't make out much about the person. I can't tell if they're male or female, old or young. But I know for certain that their eyes seared into my soul by the heat that spread across my body when my eyes found their form across the parking lot.

Snapping my eyes back to the dashboard in my car, I turn the key, bringing the engine to life before speeding away, a feeling of static much like Birdie talked about settling deep within my belly.

The winds of change are coming, Immy.

Two

Luna Sea Plaza
Owner's Chat

MAEVE: What on Earth is happening at the plaza today?

SUNDAY: Took me ten minutes to find a parking spot at nine in the freaking morning!

CAMPBELL: If any of you dared to pay attention to Watson's weekly email, you'd know the new shop that moved in is opening today.

SUNDAY: Going to need some aloe for that sick burn, Cam. We can't all be as wise and all-knowing as you are. *eye roll emoji*

CAMPBELL: Do not call me Cam.

IMOGEN: *GIF of woman hitting snooze*

IMOGEN: So you're saying I shouldn't be late today?

HOLLIS: What kind of shop is it?

OAKEN: A cannabis dispensary.

CAMPBELL: Just what this place needs. Another controversial store to drive more customers away from the toy store.

HOLLIS: I don't know. The people who buy my toys never seem to complain.

IMOGEN: *GIF of dancing vibrators that says Good Vibes Only*

SUNDAY: Seriously, CAM. Lighten up.

HOLLIS: Come by any time, Campbell. I've got some toys that would be perfect for you, too.

WATSON: Back in my day, we had to do things the old-fashioned way and entertain ourselves.

WATSON: Kids are all spoiled nowadays with all these toys and gadgets.

OAKEN: Who is going to tell him?

SUNDAY: Bless your heart, Watson.

HOLLIS: S-E-X toys.

CAMPBELL: For Christ's sake. What happened to this chat thread being for pertinent plaza-wide information only?

WATSON: Oh, well, in that case...

WATSON: Hollis, maybe I can swing by, and you can show this old dog a few new tricks to add to my arsenal for the ladies over at the retirement center.

WATSON: Shoot. Wrong text message thread.

MAEVE: Ohhhh, Watson is a dirty bird!

Three
Esme

ALTHOUGH IT HAS BEEN CLOSE TO TEN YEARS SINCE I LEFT THE sleepy, coastal town of Luna Harbor, not much has changed. The same family-owned restaurants and shops stand proudly on street corners, brightly-colored beachside bungalows dot the lanes that lead to the waterfront, and the distinct smell of the ocean's salt wafts proudly in the breeze as if declaring itself part of the permanent landscape.

It's nostalgic, reminiscent of some of the happiest days of my life. A feeling of coming home after a long vacation and finally being able to collapse into my own bed as opposed to an unfamiliar, lumpy mattress at a cheap roadside motel with scratchy sheets and too-firm pillows.

A small town, I pass much of my childhood on the short drive from my apartment to my new business. The school, community library, and playground pass in a blur as memories of the years I spent in Luna Harbor creep back to the forefront of my mind.

As they often do, every single memory that flits through my mind is filled with one face. One perfect girl with long, caramel locks and piercing, green eyes. The girl that I shared my first kiss with, the first woman who allowed me to explore her body as she explored mine in turn.

My first love.

My *only* love.

My Imogen.

Last night, I was lucky enough to catch the smallest glimpse of her as she left The Grateful Thread, and while I wanted nothing more than to run to her at that very second and throw my unworthy self at her feet, I knew I would certainly scare her away if I did.

And now, as I pull into Luna Sea Plaza, questions swirl through my mind like debris in the air during a tornado.

Will she be happy to see me?

Angry with me for leaving all those years ago when I had no say in the matter?

Is she even single after all these years?

Surely, some worthy woman has scooped her up by now. Or maybe, even worse, some lucky man? That thought sends a wave of nausea through my body, and I have to take several deep, cleansing breaths to steady myself.

The gears in my head turn, suddenly making me feel like coming back to Luna Harbor might have been a huge mistake. There is a very real possibility that Imogen won't want to see me, and even a smaller possibility that after all these years, she won't remember me.

I push the thoughts from my head as Aveline pulls into the parking spot next to where my beat-up Toyota is parked.

In her mid-thirties, Aveline is not only my best friend but my co-worker, too. We met shortly after I left home at seventeen, literally running into each other at a homeless shelter I had been frequenting. As I came around a corner with a tray of food in hand—the first warm, fresh food I would have been able to enjoy in days—I walked right into her chest, sending the tray full of creamy potato soup and warm rolls clattering to the ground around us.

Earlier that very day, I had been asked to leave the public library after an older, not-so-kind librarian found me with my head down, sleeping on a desk with several books spread on the table in front of me. I hadn't showered in a few days, felt dirty, and was seriously underdressed for a Colorado winter. Of course, I was already on edge from my run-in with the librarian, and the tray incident was the last straw I could handle before everything simply fell apart.

The second the tray hit the ground, I lost it. It had been such a difficult few weeks full of uncertainty. Full of scary situations and untrusting people. Full of loneliness and longing to belong.

I expected Aveline to be angry at me because some of the food had gotten on her clothes during the collision, much in the way it then splattered the front of my own hole-filled and frayed threads. Instead, the second I started to cry, she pulled me into her arms, holding me tight while telling me that everything would be okay. It was maternal in a way I hadn't experienced since the day my parents ripped me away from Luna Harbor after learning the truth about me.

After learning that their darling daughter was gay.

Aveline and I talked that night and almost every night after, quickly becoming friendly with one another. With almost ten years separating us, I soon began to look up to Aveline, to consider her not only a friend but an older sister the world sent my way when I needed family most.

While I had left my family out of fear of my own safety, she had escaped her own hell several years prior in the form of an abusive husband who refused to grant her a divorce. And while on paper, we appeared to have nothing in common, our stories of abuse and neglect, of running to create a safe existence and finding acceptance, brought us together in an unexpected way.

After almost half a year, Aveline and I scraped together enough money and moved into a small studio apartment together. Then, as soon as I turned eighteen, she helped to get me a job alongside her at a family-owned cannabis cultivation facility, the type of place that grows cannabis and harvests it before it is turned into various products, packaged, and sent to dispensaries.

It was long, often grueling work in the indoor grow houses

under large, artificial lights where we harvested all our crops by hand, but it allowed me to make a steady stream of income, a huge improvement over the odd jobs I was often able to get before I started working alongside my friend. The job also opened my eyes to an entire industry I didn't know existed, and I became hooked on learning everything I could about cannabis both medicinally and recreationally.

From cultivation, I moved into the small company's dispensary where I learned the customer service side of things. And while I was initially unsure of working in a position where I had to talk to new people every day—I knew firsthand how cruel the world could be—I found that I truly enjoyed getting to know my customers and being able to recommend products for them based on what they were looking to achieve.

Trouble sleeping? I had just the strain for that.

Dealing with anxiety?

Struggling with depression?

Experiencing near daily pain due to any number of ailments?

With cannabis, I was able to help people with all of those and more.

Throughout the years, I continued to save every cent I could, always hell-bent on coming back to Luna Harbor as soon as possible. And when the High Tide brand decided to branch into another state, I suggested the small town that held my best memories without hesitation, going as far as to create an entire PowerPoint about the town. I highlighted the pros of the area— the near year-long tourist season, the relatively new passing of recreational usage, the small town feel that continued to keep the family-owned vibes that were paramount to our owners.

Surprisingly, they agreed after doing research of their own, and when I suggested moving to open the location since I was familiar with the town and having Aveline come with me to get the store off the ground, they were on board, knowing how well we had worked together over the last seven years. My friend, who had never left the state she was born in, was ecstatic at the promise of seeing the ocean for the first time and at the prospect of almost year-round beautiful weather.

Aveline and I open and close our respective car doors simultaneously, and as we walk toward the shop, I suck in deep breaths full of the salty air wafting in from the nearby beach.

"Hey, boss lady," she calls out. "Excited for our first official day?"

I gently bump into her shoulder with my own. "What makes you think I'm the boss? You are older and therefore wiser."

Giving a wave to Oaken, the dude who owns the convenience store in the plaza, we unlock the door and enter High Tide as my friend's laughter echoes through the vacant shop. "That's a load of bullshit, and you know it! Besides, if it weren't for you, I'd still be in Colorado, likely freezing my ass off instead of being a ten-minute walk from the beach. As far as I'm concerned, that's enough to make you the boss lady in my books."

Slipping into the small back room we've outfitted into a break room, I turn on the coffee pot, letting the aroma fill the shop around us as it lazily drips into the glass carafe below.

We've been working through the night for close to the last week, making sure all items we ordered arrived, merchandising the display cases, and of course, testing a few of the products, too.

Quality control at its finest.

It wasn't until I started working in the cannabis industry that I became an advocate and full-time enthusiast of the plant. But after I saw the effects it had on my own sometimes-crippling anxiety, there was no way I could work in any other industry. I became obsessed with researching the medicinal benefits that pot had on different conditions, poured over case studies on different strains and terpenes, and dedicated myself to bringing awareness to the little miracle plant that has more benefits than the rocking good time it's often associated with.

The second-best thing about our new location, aside from reuniting with the woman I was taken away from so many years ago, is having a staff that is almost just as passionate about education as I am.

Along with myself and Aveline, we are opening with five additional employees and today, it's all hands-on-deck as we open our doors to the public for the first time.

Ezra and Sarah arrive first, quickly getting to work by hanging a large banner advertising our grand opening outside the store before placing several large flags along the road leading to the plaza. Eileen is next, carrying in bags of snacks and drinks for the grand opening, which she sets on a folding table that has been erected for the occasion. She pulls a gorgeous, dark green, sequined table cloth from another bag and confides that she purchased it from Etsy as soon as she heard about our plans for the opening. When I offer to pay her back, she refuses, saying that she's had her eye on the glittery cloth for months before purchasing it with no use for it until today. Aiden and Zander are last to arrive, though still on time for their shifts. The youngest of the employees at our location, they each remind me so much of myself when I first started my career as a vulnerable young girl, although they hold more confidence and swagger than I ever did at that age.

When everyone is finished with their morning tasks, I call out for them to meet me at the front door. They watch as I affix a small, rainbow flag sticker to the glass outside of our door, the words *diverse, inclusive, accepting, welcoming safe space for everyone* accompany the flag, proudly displaying our business as a space where everyone should feel welcomed. Along with my co-workers who watch me from the window, a fluffy, gray cat also observes the process, sitting on the sidewalk near the toy store that sits one door down from our shop.

While Aveline knows my entire story, including why my desire to return to Luna Harbor was so strong, it is something that I haven't broached with the rest of our employees in the short time I've known them. But I know as we continue to grow closer, they'll learn about me just like I'm learning about them, and that they will come to understand exactly why it is paramount that our store be welcoming to everyone.

I walk back into the door, producing a small, plastic tube from my back pocket. Popping it open, I slide out a pre-rolled joint and hold it out to my best friend in offering. "You want to do the honors?"

She greedily takes it and holds the tightly packed paper above her head. "I know I speak for both Esme and myself when I say that we are extremely excited to be on this journey with you. You might think this is all fun and games," she pointedly looks at Aiden and Zander, "but you have the ability to change lives by being here with us. This little plant can do so much good, can help with so many things where traditional medicine has failed. Hell yeah, it's fun as hell to smoke, but having fun isn't where cannabis's benefits end. It's up to us to not only educate our customers but also the public as a whole. We're going to do amazing things here, and I'm confident this is only the first Florida will be hearing of the High Tide brand."

Several small cheers break out across our little group, and they only continue as Aveline flips open her glittery *Zippo* lighter, puts flame to paper, and inhales deeply before dramatically exhaling the smoke and passing the joint to me.

I take a few hits before passing it along, and soon enough, everyone has enjoyed the inaugural joint of High Tide at Luna Sea Plaza, and I know it is just the first of many.

Four

Luna Sea Plaza
Owner's Chat

IMOGEN: Swear to God, I waved at Mr. Freeze on the way in today, and he glared daggers at me! We didn't get that far off-topic in the less cool owner's chat.

SUNDAY: Mr. Freeze?

IMOGEN: Campbell.

HOLLIS: Oh, that's a good name for him!

SUNDAY: I think I'll make that his name in my contacts.

MAEVE: Sometimes, I really wonder about him.

SUNDAY: Sometimes, I wonder about him naked, but then he opens his mouth and his personality ruins it all.

OAKEN: Looks like I checked in just in time.

IMOGEN: Yeah, talk about taking a ten and turning it into a two.

OAKEN: I hope we're still talking about Mr. Freeze and not me joining the conversation.

IMOGEN: *GIF of someone locking their lips and throwing away the key*

IMOGEN: Kidding, of course! Love you, Okie Dokie!

OAKEN: Uh huh.

MAEVE: I checked out the new place first thing this morning.

MAEVE: Birdie was already over there. *Laughing emoji*

IMOGEN: *GIF of someone rolling their eyes*

IMOGEN: I'm fairly confident I'm going to have to drag her out of the place.

HOLLIS: *GIF of May The Odds Be Ever In Your Favor*

IMOGEN: OMG, you used a GIF!

IMOGEN: *GIF of a woman that says Proud Mom*

Five
Imogen

WHEN I ARRIVE AT THE GRATEFUL THREAD ON THURSDAY afternoon, the parking lot is buzzing with excitement. While our little plaza generally sees pretty steady business, the energy today is ten-fold, reminding me of the hectic days leading up to a busy Christmas holiday.

More cars than I can count line the parking lot, and even more vehicles are parked in the grass that surrounds the plaza. I am lucky to have found a parking spot as quickly as I did, and I silently curse the newest tenants for the frenetic energy around the usually laidback space.

On the sidewalk in front of the new dispensary, a DJ from a local radio station plays music while customers passing by spin a giant wheel to claim free prizes. Both the station's mascot and a person dressed as a giant pot leaf mull around, joking with each passerby. A few doors down, at the end of the strip, is a food truck serving tacos, and the scent makes my stomach grumble despite the fact that I just ate lunch less than an hour ago.

There is a short brunette standing outside of the door to the dispensary handing out flyers and I laugh when I see Grandma Birdie talking with the woman, already well on her way to making a new best friend. I give my grandmother a quick wave before ducking into the quilt shop, saying hi to Allison as she measures and cuts fabric for an older woman, who is holding a bag with the High Tide logo embossed on the side. Taking quick stock of our shop, I see several customers that I don't recognize, all holding the same bag as the woman having her fabric cut.

It appears that there is more of a customer crossover from quilt stores to pot stores than I ever imagined, but knowing my grandmother, I guess I shouldn't be that surprised.

Filing away my newfound knowledge to discuss with Grandma Birdie at a later time as marketing ideas run through my mind, I toss my purse behind the counter and get to work helping to turn our new clients into return customers who will grow to feel more like friends.

I'm talking with an adorable older lady who must be close in age to my grandmother when Allison finally has a lull in customers. Excusing herself for the interruption, she asks if she can duck out for a few minutes to check out the new store.

"Go! Enjoy yourself!" I tell her. "But maybe try to drag Birdie back with you on your way back over here. Otherwise, I'm afraid we'll never see her again."

Less than a half hour passes and both Allison and Grandma Birdie return, arms outstretched and full of reusable shopping totes full of random swag branded with the High Tide logo. My grandmother has on a pair of green, plastic Wayfarer sunglasses, a temporary tattoo with the shop's logo is on Allison's cheek, and both women are wearing beaded necklaces with tiny, plastic pot leaves that jingle when they walk.

"What the fresh hell is this?" I shout playfully at them. "A quilt shop or a magazine advertisement for *High Times Magazine*?"

Birdie laughs, tossing a stress ball in the shape of a marijuana leaf at me before stepping back into her role as helpful shop keep, flitting back and forth between the customers strolling through rows of fabric that is arranged in a rainbow of colors and patterns.

I'm at the counter, checking out another customer when my grandmother appears at my side. "Honey, could you give me a hand cutting some fabric?" Dropping her voice so only I can hear her, she goes on. "I may have overindulged just a smidgen next door, and I don't quite trust myself with the rotary cutter right now."

Always the life of the party, that woman.

I laugh in response. "I think I'm going to have to head over there this afternoon and have a talk with the manager. It might be a good idea if I ask them to hold off on selling to you until you're finished for the day."

Grandma Birdie's eyes flare, something hidden beneath her green irises that I can't quite make out, but the look only lasts a second before she's rearranging her facial features into a gentle smile. "Oh, Immy, I definitely think you need to go over and check it out. In fact, I talked with the store manager when I was over there earlier, and she seemed very excited to see you."

"You talk me up too much, Gram. Always thinking that everyone is excited to meet me."

She pulls me into a silly side hug, and now I know she's high as a bird soaring over the ocean on a gentle breeze. "That's because you're simply a wonderful soul, my beautiful girl." Birdie boops me on my nose. "But alas, I think you'll get along nicely. From what I can attain, I think she plays for your team."

I cover my face with my hands in horror, groaning with embarrassment as the woman at the register stares at us.

Coming out at a young age, I was afforded a fantastic support system in the shape of my accepting family. Surprisingly, of all my family members, Grandma Birdie was the most receptive of any of them, which made our already close bond grow even stronger. She was there for me when I came to her in tears and confessed to everything that happened between me and Esme after she suddenly disappeared from my life; she was there when I stood up to my school district as a senior in high school when my school deemed it inappropriate for same-sex couples to attend prom together, and she was there when I broke off my engagement to a woman I had dated for two years without any judgment, even after I told her the only reason I was breaking it off was being something just felt off about the relationship. Deep down, Birdie knew what I wasn't saying and that was that a marriage with someone could never work because they would never have my love the way I had once given it to another. That it simply wasn't fair for me to marry someone when I couldn't give them my entire heart.

As we shared our long, often emotional talks, we spent time together in her sewing room where she instilled her love of sewing into me. Over the years, I moved on from simple pillows and patterns to clothing and intricate quilts that often took first place in state-wide quilt shows, where the best of the best from around Florida would come to display their work.

It might sound silly to other people my age, to spend my free time with hobbies mainly enjoyed by those eligible to receive social security, but when I was painstakingly piecing together patterns or focusing on sewing straight lines, the hurt of the past seemed to melt away as I engrossed myself with my projects.

Throughout it all, my grandmother has been there for every milestone and project along the way, pushing me to open The Grateful Thread and agreeing to invest in the shop as my partner in order to make the store a reality.

And through every experience we've ever had together, she's been there to gently tease me while never failing to make me laugh.

"Don't you make those noises!" she chides. "All I'm saying is she shows all the signs. Baseball cap backwards on her head, those silly expensive boots you like so much, nicely manicured short nails…"

She trails off a mere second before I can slap my hand over her mouth.

"And from that," I say amused, "you can tell she is gay?"

"Seems like what all the popular lesbians are wearing on television and that TikTok app these days."

I wave a hand in front of myself, well aware that we are holding up the line. Thankfully, Allison notices and steps in to cut the fabric for the customer who was waiting for my grandmother. "So, you're telling me—for as wise and intelligent as you are, that you believe all gay women dress the same?"

She scrutinizes my outfit for a minute, a fifties-style dress that's tight up top with a sweetheart neckline. The skirt of the dress poofs out around my hips and thighs before resting just below my knees. The bubblegum pink dress is accented with big, black polka dots, and I've accessorized it with a delicate string of pearls and kitten heels that make my calves look amazing.

"Well, I suppose not *all*. You certainly dress more like June Cleaver than anything else."

Feisty old biddy.

Secretly, I know she loves my dresses. Hell, she's been the one to make half of them for me, insisting it's a business expense as it shows off the wide selection of patterns we have available and all the various fabrics we stock to make them in. She has even gone as far as to begin to design patterns of her own, offering classes in our on-site classroom, where she teaches customers how to make their own dress, in addition to the many classes we already host on quilting, embroidering, and more. It's been a unique way to introduce an entirely new generation to sewing and I always get excited when someone new comes in for their first class.

But even with as accepting and wonderful as Birdie is about not only my unique sense of style but everything else I have thrown her way over the years, I use this moment as a teaching opportunity.

"I know you're just kidding, Gram, but stereotypes can be really hurtful sometimes. I'm sure you wouldn't appreciate some young kids coming in here and thinking that you're some cranky old lady just because of your age."

"I suppose you're right, my darling granddaughter."

Clearly, I've touched a nerve by insinuating that someone would think she was anything but the kooky hippie that she truly is.

Pushing me from behind the counter, she doesn't stop until I'm nearly at the front door. "Now go. You're the only one of us who hasn't had a chance to check out the new store!"

I have no idea why she is seemingly obsessed with sending me to High Tide. I haven't smoked since I was in college, my anxiety always getting the better of me each time I tried. "Jesus Christ, are they giving away free samples over there or something?"

"Don't use the Lord's name in vain, Imogen."

Something between a laugh and a scoff comes out of my mouth at the self-professed atheist quipping about the Lord's name being used in vain, but before I can protest, she has shoved me out the door, sternly pointing toward the plaza's newest tenants.

Luna Sea Plaza's resident stray cat walks up to me on the sidewalk, weaving back and forth between my legs, but before I can bend down to pet her, Birdie opens the door just a crack, allowing the cat to run inside the shop, where she will undoubtedly be spoiled with treats. Taylor Swift—the cat, not the singer —has been at the plaza for almost as long as we have, and most of the shop owners look out for her welfare by providing food, water, and vet care when necessary. If my apartment didn't have a strict no animal policy, I surely would have taken her home with me by now.

It only takes a few minutes to walk to the other side of the plaza where High Tide is located, and as I pass by the front of the building, I wave off the DJ trying to get me to spin his big wheel of prizes and the young man in a pot leaf costume asking if I want a selfie. While I appreciate the planning and care that High Tide has seemed to place into their grand opening, the last thing I need is another canvas tote bag that will forever live in the bottom of my pantry, where I inevitably forget it each time I go to the grocery store.

Seriously, it's like the ghosts of expired spices and free swag past in there.

The same brunette woman I saw when I arrived at work a few hours ago is still at the door, welcoming customers as they are about to enter and thanking others as they leave. Her relaxed body language and posture show me that she is actually having a good time talking to people, and it makes me happy that the new tenants seem to be as customer-orientated as we are over at The Grateful Thread.

As I approach the front door, I notice the rainbow flag sticker on the glass, and when the woman greets me, I see that her name tag not only has her name—Aveline—but her pronouns as well. Again, I can't help but notice the similarities when it comes to our apparent inclusivity between our businesses, and I find myself smiling that another business that appears to be LGBTQ+ affirming has joined our little plaza.

"Hey there!" the woman says in a cheery voice. She has a wide smile that lights up her entire face, and again, it's easy to tell that her personality isn't manufactured, yet genuine.

I return her smile while responding. "Hi to you, too, and welcome to the plaza. It's a wild and wacky place, but I wouldn't change it for the world."

Her face lights up even more. "Oh, you must be Imogen! I met Birdie earlier today, and I can absolutely see the resemblance! I'm Aveline, one of the shop managers." She points to her name tag before continuing, "Come on in. I'll give you a tour of the place."

Following her into the shop, I'm amazed to see the space that was once a jewelry store has been completely remodeled. Along the back wall, a stylish check-out desk sits, several large iMac computers lining the top. The front of the desk is made of glass, an impressive display of merchandise pulling the eyes to all of the accessories the store has to offer.

One wall has several tables positioned in front of it with an abundance of snacks and drinks, several small seating areas are spread out around the shop, and while I can see several people actively smoking, the air doesn't hang heavy and smoke-laden like I would expect. It's still jarring to see people actively smoking something that was illegal for such a long time, but as long as everyone enjoys themselves responsibly, who am I to judge?

There are several smaller display cases flanking either side of the store with what looks to be different types of products on display. One display holds delicate looking dried plants, which I know are the different types of cannabis sold. Another case holds what looks to be lotions and creams, and a third has different types of chocolates and other products that look like they can be eaten.

Being around Grandma Birdie as much as I have been in the last few years as we work next to each other, I know these are her favorites, and I gravitate to the case, thinking that maybe I'll bring her a little something special after all.

Aveline walks me through a few of the different edibles, pointing out a few that my grandmother expressed interest in earlier in flavor combinations like mango jalapeño and strawberries and cream. I pick out two packages to take back to her at the quilt shop, amazed at how big this industry has seemed to grow —no pun intended.

While Grandma Birdie has enjoyed her *special treats,* as she likes to call them, for as long as I can remember, I never really paid much attention to exactly how she was consuming the product, always assuming she was simply smoking or enjoying her special brownies on certain occasions.

With surprises for my grandmother in hand, Aveline introduces me to a few employees as we walk to the rear of the shop to check out. As I'm trying to pay at the sleek-looking registers, Aveline continues to chat with me while waving off my money. I try to insist, pleading with her and the young man who is behind the counter at her side.

About to give it one more shot, I hand my card out to her once again. "Please, Aveline, I would feel horrible if I didn't."

She seems to think about it for a second, a small smile spreading over her face as her eyes begin to shine with some emotion I can't comprehend. "I'm under strict orders to never take money from you."

Scoffing, I wonder how my grandmother managed to imprint herself on Aveline so quickly that she's now getting free products after only meeting the woman this morning. "Did Birdie put you up to this?" I ask, almost incredulously.

I look at the woman behind the counter, waiting for her answer.

But she doesn't speak.

Instead, a voice breaks through the shop, wrapping around my body like a warm blanket fresh from the dryer.

"No, Imogen. *I* gave her that order."

It's familiar, yet slightly deeper than I remember with a light rasp.

But it can't be.

Whipping around, my card in one hand, the two small packages in the other, I lock eyes with the beautiful woman standing just a few short feet away before all the items I'm holding tumble to the ground landing in the space between us. Before I can recover enough to bend down and pick up everything I've scattered, my legs give out, and I go crashing toward the ground, too.

Six
Esme

Of all the ways I imagined our reunion to play out, me catching Imogen mere centimeters from the ground was nowhere on my *Return To Luna Harbor* bingo card.

In actuality, I don't have a *Return To Luna Harbor* bingo card, but if I did, the woman I love passing out when she lays eyes on me sure as hell wouldn't be on it.

The moment her green eyes landed on mine, the color in her face completely drained. I was optimistic that she would be happy to see me, if not ecstatic. Instead, I'm now carrying her to the small break room in the back of High Tide as she stares at me with a faraway look in her eyes, as if she's searching for something that I can't quite give her.

We make it to the back, and I set her on a metal folding chair, urging her to put her head between her legs. I'm not sure if the move actually does anything to prevent a person from passing out, but I've seen it done on movies enough times to think that there must be some small kernel of truth to the act.

I grab a bottle of cold water from the staff refrigerator and kneel in front of her, pressing it into her clammy, outstretched hand.

"I'm so, so sorry, Imogen. I probably shouldn't have sprung that on you."

Self-doubt fills my head, and I'm about to ask her if she wants me to walk her back to the quilt store so I can lick my wounds in private when she lifts her head and studies me.

As her eyes trail over my face, I take the time to study her as well. Those big, green eyes that were always my undoing are still bright and clear. Her chestnut locks hang in loose waves around her shoulders, and while her facial features and body have softened with age and time, she's still as stunning as ever.

Long, silent minutes pass in the space between us, her still in the chair while I kneel at her feet like the unworthy woman that I am. Hesitantly, her hand reaches out, touching one of the curls that escaped from under my baseball cap.

"Is it really you?" she whispers while looking at me with a furrowed brow. "Are you really in front of me right now?"

I smile at her, trying to appear more unaffected at being back in her presence for the first time in nearly a decade than I actually am.

"It's really me, Immy. I'm really here in front of you."

Unshed tears shimmer in her eyes, and when one finally breaks free, I instinctively reach up and wipe it away.

God, if I could only take away the pain of what happened between us all those years ago. If I could have done something —*anything*—to not have left her without a word. She could hate me. Hell, I wouldn't even be mad at her if she did. Despite the fact that leaving Luna Harbor was *never* my decision, I can't help but be fearful that she blames my disappearance from her life on me.

Yet, she isn't looking at me now with anger or hatred or disappointment. Instead, she continues to study me as if she is cataloging every feature of my face and storing it away in some locked vault. As if at any second, I'll poof into thin air, leaving her alone again.

I know I need to take this slow, to give her time to get to know me as an adult, but all I really want to do is pull her into my arms, press our bodies together, and kiss her until we're both struggling to breathe. I'm determined to make her mine because, in all honesty, she never stopped being mine in the first place.

Still, for now, I do my best to push the desperation coursing through my body back into a small, glass bottle before tossing it out to the sea that is my whirling mind.

Reaching out, I take the hand not holding the water bottle, thankful that she doesn't immediately pull her hand from my grasp. "I have *so* much to explain to you, Immy. So many things to share with you and so much time to make up for that was lost. But for now, I just need you to know that I'm back and nothing can pull me away from Luna Harbor again. No one can pull me away from *you*."

I know she doesn't understand the implications of my words right now, but in time, she will. In time, I'll tell her exactly what forced me from her life and how every move I've made over the last ten years was strategically taken to bring me closer and closer to her again.

She lets out a light giggle that echoes through the tiny room, and the sound of it is like a soothing balm to the skin. "My grandmother was insistent on me coming over here to introduce myself. Guess now, I know why."

I give her a wry smile in return.

"Did you know?" she asks. "Did you know that The Grateful Thread was mine?"

"Not initially," I tell her truthfully. "Honestly, the plaza was the only place in town that had affordable rent when High Tide started looking to expand. I had my suspicions though. I mean, how many quilt stores could a small town have? And a name like The Grateful Thread, I knew Birdie had to have a hand in that in some way. I didn't know if you even still lived here. Didn't know if you had gotten married and moved, if you'd be happy to see me, if you'd even want to see me…" I trail off, self-conscious of overloading her with all of this so soon after reuniting.

Her cheeks are rosy from emotion, and even after ten years, she looks fucking perfect.

"I do," she says. "I mean, I am happy to see you. It's just a shock."

I smile again, so wide that it hurts my cheeks. But that's just the effect Immy has always had on me. I've been putty in her hands since the day we first met as kids, where I sat next to her in a too-tiny-for-two-people desk.

"Tell me I can take you to lunch sometime soon? It's been too fucking long."

As Imogen stands from her chair on slightly wobbly legs, I push myself up from the ground. Standing this close to her, less than a foot of distance between us, I can smell her perfume, and it takes me back to our teens with its slightly peppery yet floral smell. "Still wearing Chance by Chanel, I see?"

She laughs in response, and I wonder if she remembers the first time she smelled the perfume.

Her parents had dropped us off at the mall a few weeks before Christmas so we could complete our shopping together. Of course, we had limited funds as two teenagers shopping for their families, but when we stopped at the cosmetics counter and she inhaled the perfume, her eyes going wide with delight at the smell, I simply knew I had to surprise her with a bottle. I snuck back to the counter when she went to the bathroom and hid the bottle in the pocket of my oversized cargo shorts.

When I was finally able to give it to her, wrapped perfectly in adorable snowman wrapping paper with a little red bow, she cried and threw her arms around me as she peppered my face with kisses.

That was our last Christmas together.

"Lunch?" I ask her again.

Slowly, she nods. "Lunch would be nice."

She hands me her phone, and I input my number before sending myself a text from her cell. Handing her back her phone, we stare at each other again, almost as if neither of us can quite believe that we're actually standing in front of each other after being apart for so long.

"I should get back to the store. You know Birdie, can't let her out of my sight for very long, or she might accidentally burn the place down."

Awkwardly, we maneuver around one another, almost as if neither of us knows exactly what to do next. She moves to the left at the same time as I do before we both shift to the right at the same time. But then amid our slightly chaotic reunion, Immy laughs, making me laugh, too. Soon, we're both in a fit of giggles, wiping tears away from our eyes and acting like we did as two silly little girls on the playground at recess.

Stepping closer to me, Immy presses a hand to my forearm, sending electricity coursing through my body.

Seriously, I'm like the little kid in the original *Jurassic Park* when he gets zapped by the electric fence. Except where he was forced to let go, I'm determined to hang on for as long as I can.

"Sorry I nearly fainted on you," she says shyly. "I'm just… I'm surprised in the very best way possible."

We share a short embrace, a strictly platonic hug between two long-lost friends before I walk with her to the front of the store. I stop by the register, grabbing her card and the edibles she picked out for Birdie and tucking them into a canvas tote bag with the High Tide logo on the front. I add a few more surprises before passing her the bag, and when she takes the bag in an outstretched hand, she laughs.

"I turned down a bag from the dude who is here from the radio station out front. He's going to be pissed to see me come out of here with one of yours."

My mouth moves before my brain can catch up. "Eh, we both know I can give you more than any man ever could. Reusable totes included."

Imogen's eyes go wide, and a blush creeps up her cheeks. Brushing off my comment with a shake of her head, she replies,

"I'll text you about lunch. Come by the shop and I'll give you a tour whenever you want. It really is good to see you, Esme."

It's the first time she has said my name, and the way it soothes my tattered soul tells me that coming back to Luna Harbor was the absolute right decision.

She quietly walks toward the door, and I don't miss the way Aveline watches from across the dispensary, her eyes bouncing back and forth between Immy and myself as she raises her eyebrows in what is supposed to be a seductive way.

I have to stifle my laughter because all she does is manage to look ridiculous.

As Imogen reaches the door, she turns back toward me, flashing me a dazzling smile that sucks all the air out of my lungs.

Months bouncing between living on the streets and short stays at homeless shelters. Week after week of wondering where my next meal would come from—if I'd even have a meal at all. And yet, right now amidst the promise of seeing Imogen for lunch is the hungriest for a meal that I've ever been.

Seven

Luna Sea Plaza
Owner's Chat

> IMOGEN: I'M MEETING ESME FOR LUNCH TOMORROW!

MAEVE: A second chance love story in the making! This would make an excellent plot for a romance book.

> IMOGEN: It really is. I still can't believe she is here!

HOLLIS: I'd read the shit out of that book.

SUNDAY: Throw in a couple long, hard rods and a few velvet-covered shafts and I'm in.

MAEVE: Listen. I like dick but those euphemisms are enough to make even me cringe.

OAKEN: I'll never know how I got so lucky to be in on this chat.

HOLLIS: You love it. Don't you?

OAKEN: Fuck yeah! How else would I have ever learned what pegging was?

> IMOGEN: Can we please get back to the topic at hand?

SUNDAY: Which is?

IMOGEN: What should one wear if they are going out to lunch with the absolute love of their life after not seeing them for close to a decade?

OAKEN: Welp, that's completely outta my wheelhouse.

OAKEN: I'll let you ladies get back to it.

OAKEN: *GIF of Homer Simpson disappearing into bushes*

Eight
Imogen

ESME: Sorry to bother you so late, but I have a question about the plaza that maybe you can answer?

IMOGEN: I'll do my best!

ESME: There is a large, fluffy cat meowing incessantly at our rear delivery door. Do you know who it belongs to?

IMOGEN: That's Taylor Swift!

ESME: The songwriter?

IMOGEN: The cat.

ESME: The cat is named Taylor Swift?

IMOGEN: Yep! She hangs out around the shops, always waiting for a handout.

IMOGEN: If she's being a bother, just walk down to Buy The Way and Oaken will take her off your hands!

ESME: Thank you! Still on for lunch tomorrow?

IMOGEN: Wouldn't miss it for the world!

SMOOTHING DOWN MY DRESS, ANOTHER FIFTIES-INSPIRED STYLE covered in tiny, little red cherries, I attempt to remove as many wrinkles from the fabric as I can before opening the door to the quiet cafe I'm meeting Esme at for lunch. A quiet, little place just a few blocks from the ocean, it's one of my favorite lunch spots not only because of its location but because of their delicious coffee drinks and homemade salads and sandwiches, too.

This is Esme, my best friend, the girl I loved for years—even after she was gone. Yet, I find myself strangely nervous to be alone with her after all this time. Between our schedules and other engagements, it's taken us almost two weeks to carve out time for lunch, and my palms are clammy with anticipation as I walk to the table where Esme is already seated. She glances over the menu, chin tilting upward when I approach. A giant smile breaks out across her face, and while many years have passed, she's still as beautiful as the first day we met.

Small laugh lines form at the corner of her eyes, while two deep dimples spring to life on either side of her mouth. No baseball hat in sight, her curls hang in shaggy spirals around her face, hitting just under her chin in length. I hold myself back from reaching out to tug on one of the spirals, wanting to see it tightly recoil into its natural, bouncy form.

Before I can sit, Esme stands from her chair at the small bistro table and pulls me into a hug. Her embrace is soft and comforting, a familiar feeling that I melt into. Her curls tease my cheek, and when she ends the embrace, she simply holds me at arm's length for a moment, as if she is worried I'm going to disappear in the blink of an eye.

"Ten fucking years," she says as if she can't quite believe it herself.

I nod while taking my seat. "Ten years."

Our server comes to the table, taking our drink orders before hurrying off to collect our beverages.

This time, I'm the one to break the silence. "I'm really glad we're finally getting to do this. It's amazing to be able to catch up with you after all this time."

"Me too," she says. "You were always something else, Immy. But now, you're like a way more beautiful version of Ms. Frizzle."

I blush under her praise, half-amused that she's comparing me to the quirky schoolteacher from *The Magic School Bus* with her signature wacky dresses, while the other half of me hangs on to her calling me beautiful for the first time in forever.

Over the last two weeks, we have only seen each other a handful of times. Esme coming over to drop off some new products for Grandma Birdie to try, running into each other at the garbage dumpster at the end of our days, or quickly waving to one another as we got in or out of our cars. We've texted back and forth, our conversation mainly on Luna Sea Plaza. I've filled Esme in on the other shops and their colorful cast of characters, telling her who is friendly—basically everyone—and who isn't —Campbell, the owner of Timeless Toys. She's filled me in almost daily, recounting the often-funny stories of the customers that have come into High Tide, while I've sent her videos of our ridiculously silly delivery driver who is TikTok famous for his videos of him in the back of the truck. The guy has some wicked dance moves, and he loves to show them off to his throngs of adoring fans.

And through all our text messages, I've found myself smiling and laughing more than I have in years.

We both glance at the menu, making selections when our server comes back with our drinks. When she disappears from our table, our flimsy, plastic menus in hand, we return to our conversation.

"So, I know we have more than enough to talk about, but first thing is first—who the hell named the cat at the plaza Taylor Swift?"

I raise a hand. "Guilty as charged."

Esme laughs, and the sound is like a million little bells tinkling at once. What I wouldn't do to be able to capture that sound. She quirks a brow in my direction as if urging me to continue.

"Taylor Swift—the person, not the cat—has a cat named Olivia Benson. You know, after the character on *Law & Order: Special Victims Unit.* I thought it was only fair that since Taylor Swift has a cat named after the character, that someone named a cat after the singer in return. I know she's technically not *my* cat, but everyone else just called her Plaza Cat, and I felt she was deserving of a name. Plus, you've heard how loud the cat is, always screeching for some sort of treat. It's practically like she is singing."

Another laugh tears from Esme's side of the table. I catch her glimmering eyes with my own, smiling at the sound.

"Well," she finally says while shaking her head as if in disbelief, "I suppose there are worse names than Taylor Swift."

Nodding emphatically, I agree. "Person Taylor also has cats named Meredith Grey and Benjamin Button. So, all things considered, I think I chose wisely."

We settle into easy conversation, talking back and forth about Esme's new shop and The Grateful Thread while veering away from more sensitive topics. I can't quite tell if Esme is ready to talk about why we really met today, but I try to move the conversation in that direction.

As we pause for our server to deliver our food, I decide to take the plunge. Once we're alone again, settled with our meals —a chicken salad sandwich for Esme and a tortilla salad for me —I ask the question that has been on my mind since I nearly hit the floor at High Times. "Why did you choose Luna Harbor for the location?"

Esme pauses with her sandwich halfway to her mouth before returning it to her plate and wiping off her hands with the linen napkin that sits across her jean-clad lap. Reaching over the table, she lightly covers my hand with her own. "Because I had to find you. I knew that, if for some reason, you had moved, this would be the best starting point to find where you went."

I don't pull my hand from under hers, letting the electricity of her touch sear into my skin. Closing my eyes, I take a moment to get the rampant emotions swirling through my brain under control. "I tried to find you over the years. So many times. I tried every social media platform I could think of; I've Googled you more times than I care to admit."

She gives me a rueful smile in return, along with a small squeeze to my hand that is still tucked warmly under hers. "The last ten years haven't been kind to me, Imogen. I've stayed away from social media, tried to keep my head down, and worked toward my goals while maintaining a life of anonymity. It was safer for me that way."

Pulling her hand away, she brings her sandwich back to her face, silently signaling that she isn't ready to tell me the rest of the story just yet. While I could be untrusting of her and push for more information, one look at her beautiful face shows the pain and emotion she is hiding behind her golden, honey eyes.

Even though a decade has passed since we were so much more than friends, I want to protect her both from the pain of her past and whatever lies ahead on her journey. We may be nothing more than friends, but in some small way, she'll forever be my Esme.

We continue to talk, her regaling me with stories of Colorado and me recounting crazy times I've shared with Birdie over the years. She asks about my parents, and when I ask about her family, Esme freezes in place, a deer in the proverbial headlights of my gaze.

She takes a deep breath, seeming to collect her thoughts—or maybe her courage—before she replies, "I haven't spoken to them in almost eight years."

I gasp, dropping my fork to the table while both of my hands come up to cover my mouth. Esme must see the cogs of my brain working overtime to catch up with what she said because when she smiles at me this time, it's not playful or wry but sad with a hint of longing.

"It's okay," she says so quietly that it's just above a whisper. "It's better this way—for everyone."

Moving back into lighter territory, we talk more about work before breaking out into fits of laughter as we talk about memories of our childhood and teenage years.

Esme wipes at a stray tear that has escaped after a voracious round of laughter. "Do you remember when Mr. Barrett thought he lost us on that field trip to Disney in tenth grade?"

I howl with laughter, loud enough to cause several other diners to stare in our direction. "Oh, my God! How could I forget?! There we were, sneaking away from our group who was waiting to ride Space Mountain so we could make out on that little ride that circles Tomorrowland instead."

"Best day ever," she says wistfully.

"I thought my parents were going to kill me. My mom swore I was grounded for the rest of my life when she heard we had snuck off on our own."

Esme takes the last bite of her sandwich as I polish off my salad, dragging the last forkful through the dressing that soaked to the bottom of the large, ceramic bowl. Glancing down to my watch, a Swatch watch that has cherries on it just like my dress, I take note that I need to be at the quilt shop in less than a half an hour.

I try to pay for my half of the meal but am once again thwarted by Esme.

"What is it with you not letting me pay for things?" I ask as we make our way to the sidewalk, walking shoulder to shoulder to our cars.

Esme keeps her eyes forward, not turning to look at me as she replies, "I've been away for ten years. I have a lot of time to make up for."

Placing my hand on her forearm, I stop our slow walk to the parking lot and pull her away from the tourists dressed in bathing suits coming and going from the beach. "I have a feeling that you leaving and being away for ten years wasn't exactly your idea." Esme tries to speak, but I stop her. "Let me finish, please." She gives me a curt nod, and I continue. "I don't know what happened, and I know when you're ready, you'll tell me everything. But know that one day or ten years away, you don't owe me *anything*. You don't have to pay for my meals; you don't have to impress me or go out of your way for me. Sure, we're just getting reacquainted with one another, but Esme, you were always my best friend and that didn't stop the day you left."

She pulls me into a hug, right there on the sidewalk, and as people pass us, we stay locked in an embrace as if the world beyond our bodies doesn't exist. Before pulling away, she drops the softest kiss on my cheek, sending goosebumps over my skin despite the warm Florida weather.

"I'll see you soon?" she asks.

I give her a playful nudge with my shoulder. "Yeah, don't you close tonight, too?"

We get to our cars, surprisingly parked just a few spaces away from one another in the oversized parking lot. I'm about to slide into my car when I stop.

"Hey, Es!" I holler out before she can get in her own car.

Her eyes snap to mine over the cars standing between us.

"Welcome home!"

She gives me a dazzling smile, lighting up not only her eyes but her entire face.

Before she dips her head into her car, she calls back, "It's the only place I ever want to be."

Nine
Esme

WAKING ON SUNDAY MORNING, I THROW THE COVERS FROM MY bed while struggling to breathe. Slightly dizzy, I feel like I'm taking my first breath after being held deep under the ocean's waters with no way to reach the surface.

Looking at my phone, I groan, knowing there is no use in going back to sleep until my alarm goes off—in a measly seven minutes.

It has been years since I last had a nightmare that I can remember—one that woke me from my sleep with unease and clammy skin—and the return of what was once near-nightly torture has my stomach in all types of knots.

Cursing the memories that accompany my dream, I run my hands over my face before stumbling to the shower in the small, one-bedroom apartment I rented when I returned to Luna Harbor. It's a tiny little thing over the garage of a local couple's house, but I'm proud to call it mine. At twenty-five, this is the first time since I left home that I've actually had a space to myself, a place that I am excited to turn into a peaceful sanctuary full of warm, soft blankets, oversized pillows, and delicious-smelling candles that add to the glow of the room on quiet nights.

For now, though, until I can find the time to shop outside of using Amazon Prime, it's just me, my few measly belongings, and the bed and mattress I had delivered on the day I moved in.

I take my time in the shower, enjoying the hot spray of the water as it pounds against my skin. There were times over the past ten years when I went days without a shower, let alone a *hot* shower. Now, the hot water soothes my muscles and is something I'll never take for granted. As it beats against my skin from the faucet above, I try to let go of the nightmare, pushing it further away along with the anxiety the bad dreams often bring.

Still feeling unnerved when I emerge from the small bathroom, I hastily throw on a pair of jeans and a distressed High Tide t-shirt before tucking my feet into a pair of flip-flops and tossing a hat over my curls. Eager to get to work where I can be around my co-workers instead of alone with the silence inside my brain, I'm about to tuck my phone into my pocket and walk out the door when it vibrates in my hand.

Glancing at the screen, I smile for the first time today when I see the message.

IMOGEN: Good morning, sunshine!

ESME: You always were a morning person.

IMOGEN: I guess some things never change.

She's right about that.

Like the way my feelings toward her will never change. The overwhelming need to be close to her, to wrap my arms around her and seal my lips over hers. The need to run my hands over her smooth, bare skin as we giggle with one another beneath fresh sheets warm from the dryer. To taste her skin and to lick beads of sweat off her as we rut our bodies together while chasing our combined pleasure.

While we've talked about our past over the six weeks since we've reunited, I have been hesitant to push her to see if she believes we could have a future, too. I have discovered that she is single—thank you Grandma Birdie for coming in clutch with that information—that she has dated both women and men in the years we've been apart, and that she was even engaged to a woman named Polly for a short period of time.

That was one piece of information I could have lived the rest of my life without knowing.

Another buzz of my phone pulls my attention back to the device.

IMOGEN: You guys close at eight tonight?

ESME: You know it.

IMOGEN: We're hosting our monthly game night after we close!

IMOGEN: Can you make it?

IMOGEN: *GIF of people playing Uno*

IMOGEN: *GIF of Daria and her parents playing a board game*

IMOGEN: *GIF of Jane Lynch yelling "Let's do this!"*

ESME: Wouldn't miss it for the world. *Wink emoji*

IMOGEN: Can't wait! Bring anyone you close with if they don't already have plans. The more the merrier!

IMOGEN: *GIF of person waving*

She's so damn adorable with her overuse of exclamation points and GIFs, a total extension of her equally as warm and inviting personality she shows to everyone she meets. I've witnessed her interact with customers at both her shop and mine, from the young bro-type dudes that come into the dispensary for a little afternoon pick-me-up to the little ladies who are nearly as old as the Titanic who frequent her quilt shop. With each interaction, she shows every person what it feels like to truly be heard, and it's as refreshing to watch as it is mesmerizing. She makes every single person feel heard the way I always felt heard while we were together as kids. Hell, she still makes me feel that way to this day, even if I'm still not quite ready to tell her everything.

With thoughts of seeing Immy in person tonight occupying ninety percent of my brain, the day goes quickly, and soon, I'm walking to The Grateful Thread with Aveline, Aiden, and Zander in tow.

Grandma Birdie meets us at the door, and I give her a big hug while slipping a pre-roll into the pocket of the vest she dons over her outfit. "Little something for later," I tell her with a wink.

Aveline gives her a hug next, and then the boys follow suit, each one accepting a hug from the matriarch of the plaza in that awkward way that only comes from young men in their late teens and early twenties who still don't have fully developed brains.

Aveline carries two plates of brownies. Holding out one to Birdie, she says, "Don't worry. These are the ones with the good stuff in them!"

Birdie grabs a brownie with a whoop before replying, "Go on, go on." She says before she shoos us to the rear of the shop. "I'm just waiting on Hollis, but everyone else is back in the classroom!"

We make our way to the back, and I'm surprised to see many faces from around Luna Sea Plaza that I've grown to know over the last month and a half. Along with myself, Aveline, Aiden, and Zander, I see Maeve from the bookstore, Asher and Sunday from Magical Mystical Mayhem, and Allison who works alongside Birdie and Imogen.

As we break off from our group to say hi to everyone, Imogen enters the room, arms full of plastic grocery bags. I cross to her, taking half of the plastic bags before I follow her to a smaller table pushed against the wall of the classroom. Together, we work to pull items from the bags, filling the table with chips, crackers, dips, and spreads.

Her dress today is sleeveless with a halter tied behind her neck. Lime green in color, it has tiny dinosaurs in an all-over print and dips almost scandalously low in the front, showing off the beautiful swells of her breasts. I have to all but hold myself back from throwing my head between the curves and suffocating myself beneath her tits.

Surprising me, she throws her arms around my neck, gently pressing her body against mine.

We've hugged over the last month, we've touched each other in a strictly friends-only way, and Immy even once picked a

SEW INTO YOU   61

piece of lettuce from between my teeth when we went on one of our now weekly lunch dates.

But *this* hug.

Something feels different about it, like it is filled with promises of forever. Like she wants to get lost in it, in the feeling of my arms around her, just as badly as I want to get lost in the feeling of hers.

All too soon, she breaks away, biting her lower lip while searching my eyes. "I'm excited you could make it tonight." Quickly, she looks around the room, adding as if an afterthought, "All of you."

Hollis and Birdie enter the room carrying several two-liter bottles of soda. After they drop them off on the same table as the snacks, everyone starts grabbing plates, filling them to the brim with food.

Imogen sits next to me around the large, center table as Maeve from Black, White, and Read All Over takes the seat on my opposite side with a brownie already in hand. "Hell," she says, "with a dispensary in the plaza now, I bet our monthly snack quota is about to double."

Several board games and card games sit in a pile at the end of the table—Catan, Uno, even the dreaded Monopoly. Rifling through the pile, Aiden pulls a familiar black box from the pile, sliding it toward the middle of the table. "Who's down for Cards Against Humanity?"

"Hell yes!" Immy all but shouts. "That's Birdie's favorite!"

Birdie and all of her jingling bracelets take a seat at the table, lifting a drink up to her lips in a Ganja Grandma mug. She takes a long sip of whatever beverage she snuck into the mug before speaking. "You bet your ass it is, kid. I'm in!"

Imogen tells me that often, everyone will break down into smaller groups and play multiple games at once, but tonight, everyone has decided to take their shot at the often-dirty party game.

"Yo, Mr. A to Z," I call out to Aiden and Zander. "You guys ready to get your young asses handed to you by a bunch of people at least a decade older than you are?"

As expected, they both look at me with blank expressions, but Imogen is quick to catch on, singing a few bars of the Jason Mraz song, which earns her an equally blank stare from the youngest of my employees.

Hollis and Maeve laugh as I join in, poorly singing along before they too, jump in on our impromptu acoustic sing-a-long. We finish the chorus to a round of applause, and while Aiden and Zander join in with their own raucous whistles and catcalls, I'm still not convinced that either of them actually understand the musical reference.

Cards are dealt, and the laughter starts almost immediately. Allison wins the first round when she pairs the card *if you can't be with the one you love, love* with the card *a good sniff.* A few rounds later, I send the table into a fit of giggles by using the *AXE Body Spray* card in response to the card *TSA guidelines now prohibit* blank *on airplanes.*

My young co-workers scoff in response, prompting Asher to all but demand a shopping trip with them, which he says will make women slightly less repulsed by their general existence than they have to be now with such an oppressive odor clouding their judgments.

"You really think women are into that horrible shit? Did they teach you that in man school?" Maeve asks with a laugh.

Aiden shrugs, a small blush creeping over his cheeks, while Zander quips back with a rakish grin. "I can't say I've had any complaints. Maybe you should come over here and see what you're missing, baby."

"You'd have to be vetted by my husband, sweetie," she responds slightly patronizingly while flashing a giant diamond on her ring finger. "And while we do enjoy sharing, I always let

SEW INTO YOU   63

him have his way with my playthings. I'm sure he'd *love* that tight, little ass of yours."

Laughter roars from around the table, and while I don't know Maeve all that well, I have a feeling she is being one hundred percent honest by the sincerity on her face.

It truly is amazing how well everyone from around this little community gets along with one another despite the different backgrounds of everyone sitting in this room. And while we may be the newest additions to the plaza, it has been easy to slide into a comfortable friendship with many of the people here tonight.

Everyone is still laughing while we take a short break, refilling their plates and cups, when Birdie snags my attention away from the stunning brunette on my left, who is wiping tears of laughter from her eyes. Holding up the pre-roll I had tucked into her pocket earlier, she shoots me a wink before pointing toward the shop's rear delivery door. I excuse myself from the table and follow the sweet scent of my favorite strain—Girl Scout Cookies.

I take a seat in one of two plastic chairs that butt up to the back of the building before taking the joint Birdie offers me as she sits perched in the other chair. While she has always been the very definition of a free spirit, for as long as I can remember, she's also held some semblance of regality, too. Long, gray strands of hair flow down to her back, hair that has never been touched by color and has rarely seen heat. Today, she wears a long, flowy skirt in a bright, floral pattern and a solid white shirt with a vest overtop. When I pass the joint back to her, I notice that her hands have aged since I last saw her, but just like everything else on the woman, it has been a graceful process.

"How are you adjusting to being back?" she asks, interrupting the silence between us.

"No complaints so far," I answer with a shrug, not wanting to tell her that while everything has been great, it would be even better if I could crawl between the sheets with her granddaughter and stay there locked away from the rest of the world for the rest of my life.

"I'm not sure what wind brought you back to Luna Harbor, but I can tell that you've been through a lot over the years, dear Esme. But trust me when I say that I'm not the only one who is happy that you're home."

Home.

For years, I drifted. A couch here, homeless shelter there, a run-down apartment in the worst part of town with two, sometimes three other people. Being back here in Luna Harbor with Imogen and Birdie, with Aveline and my small yet capable staff, it truly does feel like home.

Birdie and I pass the joint back and forth several times, enjoying the deep, peppery flavor of the terpenes mixed with the hint of sweet mint and lemon. We talk and laugh as Taylor Swift —the cat, not the person—meows somewhere nearby, and while I know it's time to head back inside with the others, my body is relaxed to the point where it is difficult to move.

There are few things in life that fully sate me. A great meal, having a beautiful woman writhing beneath me as I bring her pleasure, and a fantastic high like the one I have now. I don't use it as an escape from my trauma, yet it still manages to dull the near-constant pain while elevating my life with a multitude of other positive benefits.

Extinguishing the joint on the side of the building, Birdie pats my hand with hers—a gesture that she has done since the very first time I met her as a small girl. "You know, I used to smoke because it was fun. But as I get older, I really don't know what I'd do without it. If I woke up one morning and nothing on my body hurt, I'd think I was already dead."

"Oh, come on," I tell her.

"No, I swear, sweet Esme. I used to wake up feeling like a million bucks."

"And now?"

Birdie bobs her head from side to side as if trying to search her mind for her words. "Now I'm more like a bounced check."

Finally, among laughter, we extract ourselves from the plastic lawn chairs and rejoin the group, sliding back into our respective chairs around the large, center table in the classroom. Immy flashes me a dynamite smile that makes my insides melt, and I'm an absolute fucking goner when she places her delicate fingers on my thigh and gives me a little squeeze.

"Missed you while you were gone," she quips, her fingers still resting on my thigh.

Could she be flirting with me?

Testing the waters, I lean in close, lips poised just a millimeter away from her ear. "Not as much as I missed you."

I don't miss the small shiver that runs over her body on the heels of my words, as if a cool breeze just blew across her naked skin.

Trying to act as nonchalantly as possible, I resist the urge to reach out and wrap my arms around her and instead lean back. I study her from the corner of my eye, watching as she pulls her bottom lip between her teeth. Casually, I turn my baseball hat around on my head, still watching as she releases her lip and lets out a small sigh.

Our group returns to the game, several more rounds ending in side-splitting laughter that reaches near deafening levels. As I look around the room, an overwhelming pressure builds in my chest and I find myself full of gratitude for these people whom I'm slowly starting to consider as pseudo-family.

We settle on one more round, and across the table, Zander holds up a black card, reading the words to himself before repeating them out loud.

"And to end the night, folks," he says with a dramatic flourish as he turns the card to face the rest of the table. "What makes life worth living?"

"Fuck a duck," Birdie says. "Is this a dirty party game or motivational hour?"

The table cracks up when he reads the response card that says *a little boy who won't shut the fuck up about dinosaurs,* howls with laughter when Birdie claims she played the card that reads *getting married, having a few kids, buying some stuff, retiring to Florida, and dying,* and we all but break into raucous cheers when Zander reads the final card, declaring *the clitoris* as the winner to his black card.

"Are you even old enough to know where the clit is?" Sunday from the metaphysical shop calls out above the laughter.

Maeve quickly follows suit. "If you need some help, I think I have a book over at the shop with some hyper-realistic diagrams."

Zander scoffs as the rest of the table laughs, and I don't miss the way Aiden quickly averts his gaze from the table to stack his cards into neat little piles.

Hummm, I wonder what's gotten into him tonight?

As a group, we work quickly to clean up the space—tossing empty soda bottles and chip bags into a trash bag, hiding away the games in a cabinet off to the corner of the room, and wiping down the tables.

Gradually, my fellow plaza workers excuse themselves. One by one, they trail off to their homes full of family and friends. But even with the rapidly dwindling number of people in the room, I find that for the first time in a very long time, I'm not feeling alone.

Suddenly, I realize that throughout the entire cleanup, Imogen has been firmly planted in her seat, mindlessly twirling a lock of hair around her fingers. As I often do, I take a moment to study her beautiful face, but instead of her normal wide eyes, she looks like she's almost struggling to stay awake.

"Hey," I say, dropping into a crouch next to her chair much in the same way I did on the day we reunited, "you doing okay?"

When she turns to look at me, I see a familiar, far away glassy look in her eyes, and I notice the way her features are all a little more relaxed than normal. Of course, if there is anything in the world I know, it is the look on her face right now.

This is the look of someone who is high as *fuck.*

She smiles at me, a contented little sigh leaving her mouth as she leans against the back of the chair. "Yeah, just feeling really heavy and spacey for some reason."

"Baby," the endearment slips out, but she doesn't seem to notice among whatever fog she's currently in, "when I was outside with Birdie earlier, did you have any snacks?"

"Mmmhmm," she hums. "I had three of those brownies that Aveline brought over. They were won-der-ful." She punctuates each syllable of the word with a shake of her finger in my direction. "I wanted to have one more, but then decided I didn't need any more calories. I wonder if she'll share the recipe with me so I can make them at home."

"I'm sure she will," I respond with a chuckle. "And you should never have to worry about calories because you're absolutely perfect exactly the way you are. I do think you may have accidentally had pot brownies though."

She laughs in response like it's the funniest thing she's ever heard. "No way. I don't take the pot, silly goose. I'm a good girl."

Take the pot. This woman is a riot, and she doesn't even know it.

"I'm sure you are. Want to be my good girl right now and show me how you can stand all by yourself?"

God, what I wouldn't do to call her my good girl in a different situation.

Imogen sits in her chair for several long seconds with her eyes closed, a look of concentration on her gorgeous face. Finally, she opens her eyes and looks at me with no trace of humor. With slow and deliberate words, like she has to carefully think about each one to form it correctly, she responds, "As much as it pains me to say this, I think you're right, Esme. I think I took the pot. I'm not a good girl."

Unable to keep the smile off my face, I take one of her hands in each of mine. "You're still the best girl there is, Immy. Come on, beautiful. Let me help you stand, and I'll take you home."

If we were moving any slower, we'd be moving fucking backward, but finally, I have Imogen fully standing, one of my arms wrapped firmly around her waist. I explain the situation to Birdie, who laughs while running her fingers gently through Immy's hair. "You deserve a little bit of fun, sweet girl," she says to her granddaughter before turning to me. "Take care of her for the night, will you?"

She doesn't wait for an answer, already knowing exactly what I was going to say.

Because when it comes to Imogen, taking care of her is something I hope to do not just for the night but for the rest of our lives.

I just need to make her see that I'm worth it.

That *we're* worth it.

Ten

Luna Sea Plaza Owner's Chat

HOLLIS: Another epic game night in the books!

WATSON: I'm sade to missed it gain.

OAKEN: You okay over there, old man?

WATSON: Phne scrn cracked.

SUNDAY: Maybe now you can finally get a smartphone!

IMOGEN: New owner incoming!

Esme has been added to Luna Sea Plaza Owner's Chat

CAMPBELL: Must we constantly be subjected to the utter lunacy of this chat?

HOLLIS: Ah, I adore a good word pun.

SUNDAY: Not our fault you have a stick up your ass the size of the largest dildo Hollis carries in store.

ESME: Oh wow, it's like the gang is all here!

SUNDAY: Just remember big brother is here *cough cough* Campbell *cough cough*

MAEVE: Basically, anything you say can and will be used against you.

IMOGEN: *GIF of LAW & ORDER opening credits*

CAMPBELL: Pertinent. Plaza-wide. Information.

HOLLIS: First, the fact that you skipped yet another fun event planned to help everyone stay connected and friendly with one another is pertinent plaza-wide information because it proves you really are as cranky as everyone thinks you are.

HOLLIS: Secondly, Campbell couldn't take the largest dildo I have in the shop, but I'd be more than happy to give it the old college try.

WATSON: oO my.

OAKEN: Wow.

CAMPBELL: Pertinent. Plaza-wide. Information.

SUNDAY: Yeah, yeah. We hear ya, Killjoy.

Eleven
Imogen

"Good morning, sunshine!" Esme's voice sings out from across the phone line as she draws out the words, making them sound almost lyrical. Glancing at the small clock that sits atop my nightstand, I see it's already a little after ten.

Scanning my brain, I can't remember the last time I slept in this late on my day off, let alone recall the last time I woke feeling so rested. My usually clenched jaw is relaxed, the normal morning pain in my lower back is almost non-existent, and as I think back over the night, I realize I didn't wake up once, sleeping entirely through the night.

Maybe I underestimated the power of weed-laced brownies after all.

I yawn while wiping the sleep from my eyes, aware Esme is likely waiting for a response. But before I can reply, she continues talking.

"You were in rare form last night. I just wanted to check in to make sure you were alright."

Slinging an arm over my head, I groan. "I wasn't that bad."

"Imogen, you started giving names to all the dinosaurs on your dress."

"So," I respond almost petulantly but I can't contain the small amount of laughter that seeps into my tone.

"Then you took out your little dinosaur earrings and started acting out scenes from Jurassic Park on the dash of my car."

"I did no such thing!" I tell her, although now that she mentions it, I do slightly recall my dashboard antics.

She laughs in response, and the sound reverberates deep into my bones. "Then why do I have video evidence of it?"

"You do not!"

"Mmmm, do too. It would be a shame if it ended up in the group chat of shop owners at the plaza."

"Esme," I say, my voice taking on a serious tone, "you would never."

"Wouldn't I?" she responds teasingly.

I groan again, holding the phone away from my head to confirm that I hear a knock at my apartment door. "Hold on a sec. Someone is at my door."

Padding to the door, still in my ratty old pajamas that consist of nothing but an oversized tee with several holes in the fabric, I open the door a crack, keeping the chain lock engaged. Not expecting anyone, I assume it is a delivery from the post office or a door-to-door salesman, but when I peek through the small opening, I'm surprised to find Esme on the other side.

She's wearing a faded teal t-shirt that reads *be gay, do crime* and a pair of denim cutoffs that show off her lean, long legs. Her curls are hidden under a hat again, and her skin—as almost always—is flawlessly devoid of makeup.

Esme's phone is tucked between her ear and shoulder as she balances a brown paper bag in one hand and two to-go cups in the other. "Hey there, queen of the Cretaceous period. You going to let me in or force me to stand here with gifts for you?"

Shaking away my shock, I close the door long enough to slide the chain from the lock before reopening it and ushering my surprise visitor inside. Esme surveys my apartment as I lead her to the tiny kitchen. We sit across from each other at the small two-top table, and I graciously accept the salted caramel macchiato she slides my way. Opening the bag, she pulls out several buttery pastries and sets them on an unfolded napkin before gesturing for me to take my pick. I opt for a chocolate croissant, flaky and delicious while still slightly warm in the middle.

I moan at my first bite, the gooey chocolate hitting my taste-buds as if the sweet yet savory treat was designed with my specific palette in mind.

Bite after bite, I enjoy the flavors as they hit my tongue, washing them down with a large sip of my drink. The entire time, Esme simply watches me while not touching her own drink or pastry. After long, silent moments, I break the spell she's apparently under. "Are you going to eat something or is this all for me?"

She gives me a small smile, taking a sip of her own drink which I'm certain is a bitter, black coffee. The scent of our beverages hangs heavy in the air like a familiar friend. "It's just still remarkable to me to be here next to you after all these years. I'm sorry, Imogen. Sometimes it just still feels like a dream."

I can't stop myself from reaching across the small table, placing my hand over hers. Esme's skin is soft under mine, but I know beneath the top of her hand are fingers and palms callused by years of hard work. I've felt them on the occasion when our fingers accidentally brush against one another or when we break apart after our increasingly long hugs. "Believe it," I tell her. "You're *really* here." I feel the emotion bubbling up in my throat, and I try to tamp it back down with another sip of my drink. Still, when I speak again, my throat is heavy, knotted with the feelings of lost time and all we have to make up for. "I'm really here, sitting across from you at my tiny, little yard-sale-find of a kitchen table with two mismatched chairs that I picked up off the side of the road, eating croissants and drinking coffee."

Smiling back at me, Esme turns my hand over, linking our fingers together. It's such a familiar gesture, one that we've experienced hundreds of times together in the past, yet I can't help but feel a small thrill as the electricity bounces between us, zinging around the room while making everything just a little bit brighter. It gives me the chance to feel those calluses up close, to feel the rough palm of her hand as it rests against the smooth skin of my own.

I picture those hands running over my naked body, as I have with increasing intensity over the last few weeks. How the rough texture would slide against my dimpled hips and soft stomach. The way it would feel to have her hands knead my breasts and slide between my slick thighs…

"The table suits you well," Esme says after the comfortable silence between us begins to border on uncomfortable. With the hand not linked in mine, she runs her fingers over the ceramic tiles that make up the tabletop and for a moment I wonder if I spoke my previous thoughts aloud.

"Actually, everything in here suits you well," she continues with a somewhat sad smile. "You always knew how to bring color to the world."

Suddenly, I feel exposed as I sit at the tiny table in nothing but an oversize shirt across from the fully-clothed Esme. The small bout of inadvertent praise from her causes my stomach to flutter as heat creeps across my cheeks.

All throughout my childhood, I dreamt of moments almost exactly like the one taking place in my kitchen. First, thoughts of us as roommates in college as strictly platonic friends, where we would sit surrounded by open, overpriced textbooks and notebooks filled with notes while we crammed for midterms and finals before going to frat parties together. Over time, those thoughts transformed into Esme and I as a couple, spending lazy Sunday mornings in bed together as sunlight poured through open windows, the sounds of the ocean waves crashing, and nearby kids playing as the soundtrack to our day. I spent countless hours planning our future, imagining all the adventures we would go on together, conquering the world at our feet like two modern-day explorers by day while falling into a pile of limbs and continually exploring each other's bodies by night.

As I think back over the dreams I had for us together, we hold one another's eyes, and I'm certain she can see the unshed tears I'm desperately trying to hold inside. Esme's long fingers stay locked between mine, her thumb gently tracing a line up and down the side of my hand.

My traitorous body takes her simple gesture as a sign of affection, and there isn't a single thing I can do when a familiar heat starts to pool deep in my belly. Against the cool cotton of my t-shirt, my nipples pebble, and I don't miss the slow perusal Esme's eyes make as they rake over the portion of my body not obscured by the table.

I pull my hand away, breaking our contact before wrapping both of my arms around myself as if trying to break the gentle spell we're both ensnared by.

Esme uses the time to finish her drink, standing from the chair before finding the trash can neatly tucked under the kitchen sink. Returning to the table in a few short strides, she stops in front of me before reaching out her hand, helping me to stand from the table.

In my already small kitchen, Esme's presence makes the space seem even more miniscule. We're close, so close that our chests are almost touching, yet Esme makes no effort to move. One hand comes up to cup my cheek, her thumb sweeping across my skin with a tenderness so raw that I suck in a breath, simply in search of the oxygen that has suddenly been sucked from my apartment.

"You're still my favorite rainbow," she says in a low rumble, the same thumb continuing to trace the sensitive skin of my face. "Still the brightest fucking part of every one of my days." Her thumb lightly trails over my lower lip, a sharp exhale of breath rushing out of my lungs when she does. "Even when I was in hell on Earth, your memory was there every single day. It's what got me through, Imogen. Even when you were hundreds of miles away, the thought of you was enough to ground me, to keep me going on the absolute worst days."

Esme brings her other hand to my face, and it isn't until she wipes away the moisture on my cheeks that I realize I've been crying. Several tear drops have escaped, soaking into the cotton of my shirt while leaving wet marks in their wake. I let out a small hiccup as I attempt to swallow a sob. Before the sound is fully out, Esme has her arms wrapped tightly around me, her hands running up and down my back. I feel her fist the fabric of my shirt as she holds me flush against her chest, sense her breathing in my scent as she nuzzles her face into the crook of my neck, and while my mind may be playing tricks on me, I could swear I feel the barest whisper of her lips as they ghost against my skin.

"Please." It comes out as a broken sob, a tender plea. "Please don't ever leave me again. My heart can't take it, Es. I won't survive it."

She pulls away, not enough to put space between our bodies but enough to look into my eyes, her own unshed tears dangerously close to reaching the tipping point. "I will *never* leave you again, Imogen. Do you hear me, sweetheart? *Never.*"

I nod, knowing that she is telling me the truth, that there isn't anything in the world that could pull us apart now that we're this close again.

The years between us suddenly feel like they never existed. Like there was never some deep chasm that stood between our attempts of friendship and love, never some indescribable force destined to keep us apart.

Here and now, it's just her and me and the promise of all the tomorrows we have to share with one another.

Esme leans into me, and ever so slightly, she ghosts her lips across mine. It's too short, too chaste to be considered a kiss, yet every hair on my body stands on edge from the simple connection. So fast, it's over before it even begins, and I find myself leaning closer, wanting more.

Her gaze flicks to the stove's digital clock before returning to me, a beautiful smile on her often-solemn face. "I have to head into the shop for a few hours. Can I take you out tonight?"

"A date?" I ask, sounding a tinge too eager.

If Esme notices, she doesn't call me out. Instead, that smile widens even further, her dimples on full display while her amber eyes shine. "That's what I had in mind, if that's okay with you?"

My cheeks hurt as my own smile spreads across my face. Not even caring that I sound overly excited, I answer, "I'll be counting down the hours."

Once more, she pulls me into a hug before placing a gentle kiss against my cheek. This time, she lingers for just a few seconds with the soft pillows of her lips whispering across my skin.

Crossing my small, second-story apartment, she pauses before opening the door to the outside world, turning to look back at me where I'm firmly rooted to the cool, tile kitchen floor in a mixture of awe and disbelief that I may truly be getting the second chance with the woman of my dreams.

"Pick you up at six, sweetheart."

I bite my lip at the endearment, internally squealing.

She's almost through the door when I call out to her, "Esme!"

Glancing back at me over her shoulder, she raises a questioning eyebrow in my direction.

"Tell Taylor Swift I said hi when you see her today!"

Her laughter fills the room as she shuts the front door behind her, and only once it's fully shut do I allow myself to actually squeal out loud while beginning to count down the hours until I see her again.

Twelve
Esme

STANDING IN FRONT OF MY SMALL CLOSET, I RUN MY FINGERS over the countless graphic tees that hang in a multitude of colors. It isn't that I feel like I need to impress Imogen tonight; in fact, I'm actually surprised with how easily we have fallen back into a casual friendship since I returned to Luna Harbor. But still, I want to look nice for her.

Because tonight, it is about more than friendship.

Tonight, it is about beginning to rebuild the lost love I'm confident she feels for me much in the same way I still feel for her.

Settling on a pair of black skinny jeans with a few tastefully distressed holes, I pair it with a black and white striped tee and an unbuttoned plaid shirt over the ensemble. Pulling on the one nice pair of shoes I have, a small black ankle boot, I zip up the sides before grabbing a black campaign hat from the top rack of my closet.

While my hair is on the shorter side and often covered by the plethora of hats I love to wear, tonight, I opt to leave it down under the wide brim of the hat, allowing it to frame my face with the crazy curls Imogen has always had a slight obsession with.

And let's face it. I want Imogen to be as obsessed with me as I am with her.

As I'm giving myself a final once-over in the mirror, my phone chimes from where it sits charging on my nightstand, and

I'm surprised to see that it is Robert, owner of the High Tide company, who is calling.

Outside of our weekly meeting where Aveline and I catch up with Robert on the operations of the Luna Harbor location, we don't have much contact unless it is a birthday or holiday. Apprehension begins to swirl in my veins, but I push it away and swipe my finger across the screen to answer the call.

"Hey, Bob!" I force excitement into my voice, as if it's a true treat to be hearing from him, all the while alarm bells silently ring around me.

His slightly gruff voice cuts through the noise around him, and from the gentle whirring of the filtration system on the other end of the line, I can tell he is in one of the company's grow houses. "Esme, dear, is everything okay in Florida?"

Robert and I have known each other since the day I started with High Tide. In those years, I've been to his house for holidays, have shared birthday dinners with his family, and grown to consider him a pseudo-father so very different than the man who actually makes up half of my DNA. In all those years, he has never once called me dear. The endearment throws up even more red flags.

"Everything is fine here. Is everything okay *there*?" Any false pretense of excitement is gone, replaced with a sinking sensation that I'm about to hear something I desperately do not want to hear.

"Yeah, yeah, everything is good. I just wanted you to know that a woman came into the store today. Older broad, probably a little younger than me. Anyway, she was talking to Bernadette and asked about you. Said she heard that you worked for High Tide and was wondering if she could see you. Thankfully, I was there to intervene before she gave her any details—Lord knows that girl can't keep her mouth shut—but it seems like someone is looking for you, Esme. I can't be certain, but from the hair and eyes, I'd wager a guess that it was your mother."

I let out a sigh, rattled yet unsurprised that after all this time, my past seems to be catching up with me right as I'm finally truly putting it behind me.

Thanking Robert for the heads up and promising him that I'll be okay, I hang up and resume staring at myself in the mirror. Though this time, instead of looking at my outfit, I stare at my reflection in a daze as if looking through the glass instead of at it.

My palms are clammy while the tiny hairs on the back of my neck stand on end. It's hard to breathe, and again, I find myself stuck under the frequent imaginary ocean of water, struggling to make my way to the surface. I force myself to really look at myself in the mirror, to push the panic of the past away, and focus on being exactly where I am in this moment.

As I've learned to do over the years, I give myself one minute to worry. One minute to get up in my own feelings before pushing them back inside to focus on the present. Slowly, I count to sixty, inhaling through my nose before pushing deep exhales out through my mouth. I silently repeat my own personal mantras as I count, a combination of *your family cannot hurt you anymore* mixed with *you are valid exactly as you are* with a sprinkling of *you are safe and surrounded by love* mixed in for good measure.

I'm too familiar with overcoming panic, with talking myself out of a downward spiral before I completely tailspin. I used it as a survival tactic while in and out of shelters, and in part, I have the tumultuous relationship with my family to thank for that. But every now and then, even the strongest of us crumble.

I still hold on to their abuse and hatred, their vitriol and unwillingness to accept who I was as a human on the most basic of levels. I have their shame and disgust, their loathing and resentment.

There was a time in the not-so-distant past that I hated myself when I looked in the mirror. The only thing I was capable of seeing was what they saw—a woman who went against their

God, who was willing to sacrifice an eternal life in heaven for an afterlife bound to the gates of hell because I chose to lay with another woman. I saw myself as the hateful slurs I was called by the very people who gave me life, and at times, I truly thought that something was wrong with me, that I didn't deserve to exist in this world. How had an infallible God created me in his eyes to be queer if being queer was a sin? How could the very people who were so closely tied to the church, who preached love and understanding, be so completely filled with hate instead?

I had fallen in love.

They found out.

And out of that love, their hatred for me sprouted.

Time after time, hateful word after hateful word, I was pushed closer to the edge of an invisible cliff, never knowing exactly when I would topple. At times, I welcomed the edge of that cliff, inching myself closer and closer while silently praying to a God I wasn't sure existed to send a strong breeze, pushing me past the point of no return. Other times, I simply flirted with the edge, waiting for the inevitable vines that wrapped around my body, pulling me back to safety before it was too late.

My life had gone from a picture-perfect fairytale to a deep, putrid tunnel of darkness with no end in sight, and I knew that if I stayed with my family, the darkness would win and consume me whole, that I would stop flirting with the edge of the cliff and instead fall over the edge once and for all.

For days, I planned while trying to lay low around my parents. I snuck off to pawn shops and thrift stores, selling any possession I could get my hands on that wouldn't be missed. When my parents were asleep late at night, I silently snuck into the kitchen, stealing the case of good, silver utensils—the kind that tarnish and need to be polished, the ones that only come out on the most special of occasions. I hid pearl earrings in my back-pack, designer clothing under my street clothes, and my father's prized baseball cards within the pages of my books.

It took nearly two weeks of pickpocketing my own family, but finally, the night came for me to take the next step in my plan. Everything I could fit inside a single backpack and duffle bag was unceremoniously stuffed inside, the bags hidden behind piles of clothes in my ever-messy closet. Feigning illness when it was time for our Wednesday night church service, I was able to convince my mother to let me stay home. I was scheduled to work in the children's church during service, and she agreed it wasn't worth spreading illness to the littlest members of the congregation. Once she and my father had left for the evening, and I was sure they weren't coming back, I pulled my bags from the closet and took one last look at my room.

With tears in my eyes—a combination of sadness and hopefulness—I pulled my quilt from the bed. The same one I made with Imogen the summer we first met, at the time, it was like a well-worn cardigan, slightly tattered in places while threadbare in others. Clinging it tightly to my chest, I walked down the stairs, out the front door, and left my prison behind, determined to use the warm layers of fabric as my north star, destined to find Imogen again.

The same quilt catches my eye now in the reflection of the mirror and pulls me out of the haze of memories. Even more worn now, it has served its purpose, bringing me back to the woman I love, but despite its years, I refuse to part with the memories wrapped around its layers, much like the meticulous design quilted in the fabric.

I brave one last glance in the mirror, slowly...*finally*...beginning to love the woman that is looking back at me before getting in the car and driving to pick up the woman that I never stopped loving after all these years.

Thirteen
Luna Sea Plaza
Owner's Chat

IMOGEN: *GIF of Betty White saying I don't know what to do*

IMOGEN: *GIF of drag queen screaming*

IMOGEN: *GIF of red alarm flashing*

SUNDAY: Everything okay over there?

IMOGEN: Esme and I have our first date tonight.

OAKEN: How many times must I tell you that I'm trash with fashion?

HOLLIS: If fashion advice is what you seek, I am here to help.

HOLLIS: However, can we also talk about hosting a drag show in the parking lot at some point?

MAEVE: How the hell did you go from fashion to drag?

MAEVE: Actually, scratch that. Going from fashion to drag is an easy leap.

HOLLIS: The GIF from Giffy McGifferson up there gave me the idea.

IMOGEN: *GIF of Jeff Goldblum saying who me?*

SUNDAY: Where are you ladies going?

> IMOGEN: I have absolutely no idea. It's a surprise.

> IMOGEN: She did say casual though.

OAKEN: Whenever she sees you at work, you're in one of those cute little dresses that you love to make. Maybe wear something she normally wouldn't see you in.

HOLLIS: I like this idea. Something to show off your curves!

SUNDAY: And you say you know nothing about fashion, Oak!

OAKEN: I just know I like to see different sides of a beautiful lady.

HOLLIS: Oh, I'll show you a few different sides anytime you want.

SUNDAY: HOLLIS!

HOLLIS: He knows I'm just playing.

MAEVE: Probably gave the poor guy a half chub!

SUNDAY: MAEVE!

OAKEN: Goddamn…

> IMOGEN: Once again, you've all been no help at all.

> IMOGEN: Except you, Okie Dokie.

OAKEN: I…um…yeah…

SUNDAY: Great. You guys broke him.

Fourteen
Imogen

As I'm locking my apartment door behind me, ready to make my way downstairs to wait for my long-anticipated date, Esme's voice startles me. "Not even going to let me pick you up at your door?"

I turn around in the small landing space of the second story apartments, coming face to face with the most beautiful sight I've ever seen.

Esme is dressed more formally than normal, yet it's a casually chic outfit that only she could pull off. In her arms, she holds an oversized bouquet, and when she turns it toward me, I gasp, seeing that it's not only bursting with colorful blooms but that several paperback books are tucked into the bouquet as well. At second glance, all the books are ones I would have chosen for myself. In fact, each title is one that has been on my list of books to read from both seasoned and upcoming authors.

I stare at her in wonder. "How did you know I've wanted to read all of these?"

Sheepishly, she shrugs while passing the bouquet off into my waiting arms. "Admittedly, I had a bit of help from Maeve."

Unlocking the door I locked less than a minute earlier, I usher Esme inside, finding a vase and filling it with water before carefully snipping the stems and arranging the blooms into a colorful spread that brightens up my already lively apartment. Strong scents of peony and freesia fill the air, making the apartment smell like a fresh, spring day. "This is absolutely beautiful," I tell her after stepping back to admire my handy work. Piling the books into a neat little stack, I run my fingers down the carefully aligned spines while already excited at the prospect of digging into one later. "Nicest thing anyone has ever done for me."

She smiles at me before extending a hand out toward me. "You deserve nothing but the nicest of things, my love. Ready to have a bit of fun?"

My tummy flips, and somewhere deep inside, I feel that innate static that Grandma Birdie once told me about. Of course, when it comes to Birdie, I never know how much of what she says is rooted in truth, but for some reason, whatever I'm feeling right now speaks to promises of the future. Of big dreams and adventures.

Willingly, I slide my hand into Esme's, relishing in the warmth of her slightly larger hand enveloping mine. While it is a tight fit, we walk hand-in-hand down the narrow stairwell, not stopping until we reach Esme's car. She walks me to the passenger side, opening my door for me before gesturing with her outstretched palm to sit. Once I'm carefully seated, she rounds the car, sliding behind the driver's seat with graceful ease.

Somehow, she manages to even make such a mundane move look sexy.

And then, she reaches across me, pulling my seatbelt snugly across my chest, locking it into place as if I'm the most precious thing to ever exist on this planet.

Keep your cool, Imogen. Do NOT throw yourself at her this very instant and demand she take you back upstairs to screw you silly into the next century.

She lingers for just a second while pulling the belt taught across my chest, her hand barely grazing the fabric of my shirt. I'm a bomb ready to detonate from the simple brush of contact.

Esme drops her hand to the black cigarette pants I have on,

tapping one of the little bumble bees that are embroidered in an all over pattern. "I thought those were polka dots, but I should have known you would never dare wear something as plain as polka dots unless they were big and bold."

Turning on the car, ABBA's *Dancing Queen* plays softly over the stereo, and I reach for the volume dial to turn it up.

"Wait!" Esme says, but it's too late.

The sound blasts into the small cabin of the car, nearly rocking us back and forth as the lyrics swirl into the air around us.

You are the dancing queen
Young and sweet
Only seventeen
Dancing queen
Feel the beat from the tambourine, oh yeah...

I laugh, singing along until Esme turns off the car, pauses for a beat, and turns it back on—the music now soft as it was when she first started the vehicle.

"Don't laugh. The volume only works on low or max. Then, the CD got stuck in the player a few years ago. I've tried everything to get it out, but it's always *Dancing Queen*. No radio. No silence. Over and over and over again with the damn tambourine. It won't even play through the entire CD—it's like an eternity in hell with *Mama Mia* being the only movie available for rent."

We talk and laugh as we drive through the streets of Luna Harbor, the sun still overhead in the sky. Esme makes several turns, leading me down familiar streets until we pull into an equally as familiar parking lot.

I turn toward her in the tiny front seat, squealing with excitement. "Oh, my gosh—Flannigan's? Are we really to be trusted to play putt-putt together? I'm confident that last time we were here, we were explicitly asked never to return."

Esme throws her head back in a full-on cackle. "That's because you broke the window on the Snack Shed!"

Pushing open her door, Esme is at my side before I can exit the car on my own, holding her hand out to me again.

"The only reason that happened is because *you* dared me to chip my ball into the planters in the window!" I say as I take her outstretched hand.

She pulls me from the seat with ease, and I find myself wrapped in her strong arms on slightly unsteady footing. "Like you never dared me to do anything that got me in trouble," she says in mock indignance.

Feigning ignorance, though I can recall many such dares off the top of my head, I shake my head. "I have absolutely *no* idea what you're talking about Esme."

With a simple movement, she twirls me around, my back flush to her chest. Her fingers come up to squeeze my sides, making me squeal with laughter. The world around us falls away —the families coming and going from the entertainment complex, the gulls flying overhead as they search for their next French fry to steal or person to unsuspectingly shit on. Here and now, in the middle of the Flannigan's gravel parking lot, it's simply the two of us in a bubble of memories as we laugh and giggle into the warm, early evening air.

Esme finally lets me come up for a breath, tears in my eyes from laughter. As she leads me to the small building, she lists off dares that I managed to talk her into over the years, all of which got at least one of us into trouble.

"There was the time you dared me to sneak into the R-rated movie with you, only for Birdie to catch us because she was there with her sewing circle. I believe she made us do her yard work for a month. Then, there was the time we skipped school and got caught going to the beach, or the time your mom busted us for smoking cigarettes on their patio after we thought everyone had gone to sleep. And don't forget about the time you dared me to streak across the soccer field during the boy's state championship."

"You are full of shit; that was *you* who dared *me* to do that!"

She laughs, the sound bright and loud. "Yeah, I still can't believe you actually did it."

Craig Flannigan waves us to the counter, smiling when recognition hits him. "If it isn't the Tweedles," he says, referring to the somewhat creepy twins from *Alice in Wonderland*. I'm not sure if I should laugh or be embarrassed by his nickname for us, so I choose a slightly forced laugh as I give the older gentleman a small wave.

A pinnacle of Luna Harbor, Flannigan's has been around for more years than I've been on this earth. What started as a small drive-in restaurant, where servers delivered orders on skates, morphed over the years to include the Snack Shed, mini-golf course, batting cages, and an old-time ice cream parlor.

Just thinking about their banana split is enough to have my mouth watering.

"I trust you two won't be breaking any windows tonight," he says as he passes us each a golf club while eyeing us suspiciously.

In near unison, we reply, "No, Sir."

He hands Esme a folded paper scorecard and small pencil with the name Flannigan's printed across its wooden surface. She tucks them into the pocket of her shirt before leading me to rows of golf balls arranged in a rainbow of colors. With her hand settled warmly against the small of my back, she urges me to choose a color. I settle on the bright pink ball before Esme reaches out to grab a yellow golf ball for herself.

"Yellow?" I ask, somewhat surprised. "I thought for sure you would have gone with the light blue. It was always your favorite color."

She smiles, as if the fact that I remember such a small detail about her brings her great satisfaction. "Still is," she responds. "I just wanted to match those adorable little bees on your pants."

We make it uneventfully through the front nine holes of the

course, laughing and recounting stories along the way. Several times, we stop to let other families and groups play through, content to take things slow while we leisurely enjoy our time together. One would think with as much time as we've been spending together lately that we would run out of things to talk about, but with Esme, I don't think that could ever be true.

Pausing after the ninth hole, we tally our scores, only to find that we're locked in a tie.

"Care to make things interesting?" Esme asks, tossing her ball into the air and catching it with finesse that shouldn't be erotic but somehow has me feeling all tingly.

I playfully arch an eyebrow in her direction, always ready to take on a challenge. "What did you have in mind?"

She runs a hand over her face as if in careful contemplation, but the wicked glint in her eyes tells me she already knows exactly what the stakes will be.

"If you win, I'll wash and clean your car for you every week for a month. If you're still anything like the Imogen that I grew up with, you're surely leaving empty water bottles and snack wrappers all over that adorable, little, red Bug of yours."

She's not wrong.

"And if you win?" I ask her with bated breath.

Staring into my eyes, it's as if she can see every corner of my soul. "If I win, I get to kiss you goodnight at the end of our date."

I must bite my lip without realizing because Esme reaches out and pulls it from between my teeth, all the while holding my eyes with her own.

A small eternity passes between us as we simply look deep into each other's eyes. She's still beautiful after all these years, and while the prospect of kissing her, of finally reclaiming what I for so long felt was mine, is exhilarating, it's also as terrifying as getting behind the wheel on your own for the very first time.

Excitement wins out, and I drop my gaze to her lips for a

moment before returning to the soulful eyes of someone so much older than their years. With two simple words, I see a spark ignite in those amber eyes. A spark of competitiveness, of playfulness, and most of all—a spark of lust.

"You're on."

We careen full speed ahead toward the back nine, playfully knocking into one another as we try—and spectacularly fail—to maintain the lead over one another. I pull into the lead, only for Esme to come back and sink a hole-in-one on the next hole. She celebrates with a little dance, her curls wildly blowing in the breeze as they escape from around the wide brim of her hat. She points at me with her club. "Those lips are going to be mine, baby."

Baby.

We never really had nicknames for one another growing up, too young to be focused on the small intricacies that make up a person to give them something so sacred, but at this moment, I like the way baby sounds as it spills from her lips.

I like it even more because she is talking to me.

On the next hole, I come in at one under par, making it past the diabolically tricky windmill and into the hollow hole on the artificial putting green in only three strokes.

Back and forth, again and again, we take turns trailing one another through increasingly tougher holes until we come to our last chance, miraculously tied up once again.

Esme approaches the green first, carefully setting her little yellow golf ball on the turf. It's the trickiest of all the holes, designed for patrons to either hit it into the hole or have their ball meet a grim, watery demise.

Her first shot is long, mere centimeters stopping her ball from careening into the too-aqua-to-be-natural water that surrounds the hole. Lining up with the ball while teetering on the edge of the green, she brings her club back, gently tapping it in the direction of the hole. Slowly, so slowly, the ball inches toward the hole, its trajectory neatly laid out in front of it. The tiny ball hugs the curve of the hole, spinning around and around before coming to a stop on the very edge—close enough that a stiff breeze would certainly send it into its final resting place. A true, *are you too good for your home* moment, the likes of which haven't been seen since the year *Happy Gilmore* came out in theaters.

Walking to where the ball is perched precariously on the edge, Esme taps it in, the audible sound of the ball hitting the hollow hole echoing into the small space before it rolls off to the ball return at the start of the course.

I take my spot next, lining my ball up before taking a few cautious practice swings. "So close to a nice, clean car. I can almost smell that fresh-car scent of leather conditioner mixed with musty old vacuum!"

"So confident, are you? Two or less to win, Imogen."

Hitting my ball, I watch as the bright pink sphere rolls and rolls, quickly gaining speed as it heads toward the hole. At the last second, it veers to the right, coming to a stop about six inches from the hole.

I don't look at Esme, but I can feel her body visibly tense as she sees how a simple tap will win me the bet.

Walking slowly to my ball, I take a deep breath as if centering myself. Bringing my club back just a few inches, I move with forward momentum.

Closer, closer, closer.

Fuck it.

Gripping the club tighter, I slightly turn the head at the last minute, catching the ball on its side instead of straight on. Looking up, I lock eyes with Esme just as the familiar sound of the ball hitting water breaks between us.

"Whoops," I say.

She smiles, a megawatt grin that belongs in a television commercial for extra-whitening toothpaste.

Striding toward me, she quickly eats up the space between us until she is directly in front of me. She drops her club to the ground before wrapping her arms around my waist, a delicious warmth radiating out from her touch. "If I were a smarter woman, I would almost be thinking that you want me to kiss you at the end of the night."

The lights around the course flicker on, welcoming the moonlight like an old friend as the gentle sound of their electricity whirrs through the air above us.

But that's not what is electric about this moment.

With my free hand, I skate up the side of her neck until I'm cupping her cheek. Esme leans into the touch, like it is the very place she is meant to be. Letting my own club drop to the ground next to hers, I remove her hat before pushing a few stray strands of hair behind her ear.

We stare at each other as families play on the course around us. In the distance, I can hear music playing from the Snack Shed, and while I can't make out the tune, I know whatever it is, it's the perfect backdrop to this moment.

"What if I don't want to wait until the end of the night?" I ask, a slight tremble in my voice.

Before she can respond, I press up onto my tiptoes, capturing her lips in mine. It's as soft and tentative as the first time we kissed at ten years old, only this kiss is filled with lost love and promises for the future. One of Esme's hands comes to tangle in my own hair, her fingers closing into a tight fist among my tresses as she walks me backward to a nearby palm tree, lips still sealed over mine.

She breaks the kiss for only a millisecond, long enough to look at me with a lazy, satisfied grin. "Christ, Immy. Your lips taste even sweeter than I remember."

Then, her lips are back on mine.

I meet her eagerly, our lips parting to give each other

entrance, and when her tongue gently touches mine, I'm transported to another time and place all together.

A place where we were never torn apart.

A place where we've spent every day of the last ten years together.

A place I desperately hope we can return to.

It feels like hours pass, yet we're unable to let go of one another. Through gentle hugs, innocent giggles, simple kisses, and more passionate tangling of lips and tongues, we stay firmly rooted together, my back against the palm tree in the warm, Florida evening.

"Tweedle Dee and Tweedle Dum, please report to the Snack Shed immediately. Or at least stop making out until you reach the privacy of your home. There are children here, ladies."

The voice comes over the venue-wide PA system and is enough to break us apart. We fight laughter while we retrieve our clubs, still laying haphazardly on the green where we left them before walking hand-in-hand to the Snack Shed.

"You would think that being in my mid-twenties would have me less terrified of Craig," I tell her.

She laughs, giving my palm a gentle squeeze. "Better wipe that beautiful blush off your face, or he'll know exactly how embarrassed you are."

I bury my head in her chest as we approach the counter, passing our clubs back through the tiny window and into Craig's outstretched arms.

"You two are just as crazy about each other as you were when you were teenagers," he says, a look of nostalgia passing across his aging features. "Now get outta here, girls. I hear there is a banana split waiting at the ice cream shop with your names on it."

Fifteen
Luna Sea Plaza
Owner's Chat

HOLLIS: I'm waiting with bated breath over here!

MAEVE: Yes! Full details, please!

HOLLIS: They're probably having dirty, hot, filthy sex, and we're interrupting.

SUNDAY: Clearly, we all need to get laid more often.

OAKEN: …

HOLLIS: You offering up your services, big guy?

MAEVE: Mmm, Sebby would love that.

OAKEN: That's a hard limit.

MAEVE: Don't knock it until you try it, babe.

SUNDAY: You're all awful.

IMOGEN: Just walked in the door!

IMOGEN: It was MAGICAL!

IMOGEN: She took me mini-golfing where we used to go as kids. Then we shared a banana split and finished the night with a walk on the beach.

HOLLIS: Don't leave us hanging, I know that isn't everything!

IMOGEN: We kissed.

HOLLIS: And...

IMOGEN: We've decided on taking things slow.

IMOGEN: It's been ten years, and while I feel like I can pick up right where we left off, we still have so much to learn about the women we are now and how we will work together.

MAEVE: The very opposite of the traditional lesbian manifesto.

IMOGEN: You know how I feel about stereotypes. *eye roll emoji*

MAEVE: I'm kidding, I'm kidding!

IMOGEN: I should lock you and Birdie in a room together until you learn to rid them from your normal thought patterns.

MAEVE: We'd get in way too much trouble together.

IMOGEN: You're probably right.

OAKEN: Honestly, Imogen, who cares how fast or slow you take things?

OAKEN: Are you happy?

IMOGEN: Extremely.

OAKEN: Then that's all that matters.

OAKEN: Goodnight, you gorgeous group of gals.

SUNDAY: Night!

IMOGEN: *GIF of Elmo waving*

Sixteen
Esme

EVERY DAY FOR NEARLY THREE WEEKS, I'VE WOKEN UP SMILING at the sun. While I was initially worried that my reunion with Imogen was the catalyst to the return of my nightmares, after our night at Flannigan's, they've all but stopped, and I've been able to wake up feeling rested and hopeful for the future.

Immy and I have moved cautiously slow since our first date, but every day we sneak away at some point, finding any extra second where we can share sweet kisses and gentle touches.

I've kissed her in the small break room of High Tide, and she's surprised me by tugging me into the classroom at The Grateful Thread, sealing her lips over mine in a desperate show of need. With each and every day, I feel my own need to get my hands on her bare skin growing stronger and stronger.

Hearing the chime above the door to High Tide give out its signature little three note tune, I turn, half expecting to find Imogen and only a little disappointed to see Maeve instead. "Hey neighbor!" she says with a small wave as she comes up to the counter I'm standing behind.

It's a little slow for a Wednesday afternoon with only two customers currently shopping. Three others sit casually around a table, laughing and smoking while making plans for the upcoming weekend, a board game on the table in front of them.

While there are many aspects of my job that I love, seeing people socialize in a space I helped bring to life is one of my favorites. It wasn't long ago when even medical cannabis use was illegal, and to know we've come to a place where people can now smoke openly in spaces like High Tide—both medically and recreationally— is overwhelming in the very best of ways.

Aiden walks onto the sales floor from the back, takes one look at Maeve, and turns swiftly on his heels, retreating to the break room without as much as a hello. He's been shy around the beautiful bookstore owner recently, and from the light blush that spreads across his face whenever he spots her, I'm confident that he is fighting at least a tiny, little crush on the woman.

"What can I do for you, Maeve? Already out of those edibles you like?" I ask.

"Actually, I just stocked up yesterday! I wanted to talk to you about the annual parking lot party that I'm planning, *Luna Sea Lunacy*!"

I laugh at the name, knowing it's pretty spot-on for our little slice of Luna Harbor. "Tell me more."

"It's the biggest plaza-wide event we do each year, usually in late June. We bring in food vendors, musical acts, kids activities —the whole nine yards! We keep the shops open the entire day so customers can shop, and I set up an awesome scavenger hunt that winds between all our businesses. In the past, we've seen between a thirty to forty percent increase in sales for each shop on the weekend of the festival." I can see how important the party is to her from the pride in her voice when she explains all about the weekend, talking as if it is her child and she's the proud mama. "You don't have to participate, but we'd love to have you. Of course, Birdie is on the party committee with me, so you know it's bound to be a fun time!" She finishes her pitch on a sing-song note, as if dangling Birdie in front of me is a sure-fire way to get me to agree.

Which, of course, it is.

Honestly, it sounds like a fucking blast, and I tell Maeve as much. "You had me at *food vendors,* but Birdie is definitely the icing on the cake. Let me know what I can do to help out."

"Cake! That's a great idea!" Maeve quips. "We should definitely get a dessert vendor this year. Maybe someone who can tailor cake flavors to each of the shops! Oh, I can see it now! A cannabis cupcake for your shop, maybe something with a smoky vanilla undertone to represent the smell of a used bookstore for me, confetti cake for the toy store..." She ticks off each flavor as she recites them off the top of her head. "See? You have to join us for the first party planning committee meeting next week!"

Her eagerness is infectious. "Party planning committee. Now I feel like I'm at Dunder Mifflin instead of Luna Sea Plaza," I say.

Maeve laughs, a boisterous, loud sound of someone who is completely comfortable with themselves. "I love that show! My hubby is definitely the Jim to my Pam—only if the coveted office pairing were into BDSM and sometimes inviting Angela and Dwight into their bed."

Well, that is an image I didn't need in my head.

Aiden comes back to the floor, no doubt hearing the tail end of that conversation. He averts his gaze from where Maeve and I stand.

Yep, he's totally got it bad for her.

I shoot Maeve a wink before I continue our conversation. "Of course, I have some extra muscle around. If you need some big, strong men, I'm sure Aiden and Zander would be *more* than happy to help with setup and breakdown."

The nineteen-year-old glares daggers at me while Maeve simply laughs. "I've got a few more stops to make to get everyone else on board, but I'll be in touch. I'm sure Campbell will be a pain in my ass as he always is."

"He's the Timeless Toys owner, right? Imogen has mentioned him a few times. What's his deal?"

"Honestly, I have no idea. He mostly keeps to himself, and I don't think any of us know much about him. Anyway, I'll text you about next week's meeting."

She reaches the door and calls out to Aiden. He visibly stiffens for a moment before slowly lifting up his head to meet her gaze across the store. Maeve doesn't say a word, but I watch as her eyes trail over Aiden's body, starting at his face and traveling languidly down his torso and legs before repeating the process in reverse. Before turning to leave, she shoots him a little wink, leaving him even more flustered than he already was.

"Get over here, kid."

Aiden comes over to where I am standing, and I pull him into a loose headlock, running my hand over his head, messing up his hair. Out of earshot from the people still in the store, he pulls away while speaking. "You're legit like what...six years older than me? That hardly makes me a kid."

"Forget that. I didn't mean it negatively." I roll my eyes at him. "You need someone to talk to?" Changing my voice, I try to school my tone into something between friendly and maternal.

Averting his gaze, he looks at anything but me while giving me a lackluster shrug.

When we first opened, I didn't know much about my staff, but over the last few months, I've learned that while he often projects confidence, Aiden is surprisingly shy. While he may have started out as my employee, I've grown fond of the young man, and I can't help but sense there is something just under the surface dying to escape.

"Come out back with me for a minute." It's more of a command than a question, and the teen willingly follows. I ask Aveline to cover the floor for a few and usher Aiden outside.

A small, gravel patch of land sits nestled between where High Tide butts up to Magical Mystical Mayhem in the rear of the plaza. An old, wooden picnic table is anchored to the ground, and several potted plants bloom, one in each corner of the space. From the lone tree in the area, a birdhouse hangs in the shape of a cat—not creepy at all.

We sit at the splintered table, me like an actual human while

Aiden sits across from me, folded into a human pretzel. Sparking my lighter, I light a joint, passing it to him once I take a few hits of my own.

Aiden doesn't try to speak, and for several minutes, we simply sit in the quiet afternoon as the sun beats down on us from above while we pass the joint back and forth. Finally, I break the silence, still not exactly sure which way to begin. "Do Maeve's actions bother you, or is something else happening? You know, if she is making you uncomfortable, all you have to do is talk to her, and I'm sure she'll stop."

He lets out a long sigh, eyes dancing everywhere but never landing on my own. "Yes. No. I...I don't know. I mean, yeah, she makes me uncomfortable. But I *like* it."

"There is nothing wrong with that, you know. As long as you consent to the behavior. You're both adults, and sometimes harmless flirting can be fun." Aiden scoffs, like I have no idea what I'm talking about. "I'm serious, dude. You're an objectively good-looking nineteen-year-old."

That gets his attention and a smile breaks out across his face. "Objectively good-looking? I'm hot as hell, and we both know it."

We both laugh, and I give him a little nudge across the table. "Oh, yeah. You'd totally be my type if I were into men."

But then, he goes quiet again.

"What if her flirting isn't exactly what I like about it?"

I quirk a brow in his direction, silently telling him that he can continue to talk if he wants.

"Sometimes, when she talks about her hus…"

We're cut off when a delivery truck pulls into view, the back of the truck noisily rolling open to reveal rows and rows of boxes in all sizes. The smell of cardboard wafts from the rear of the truck while music blares from the front, some old Jonas Brothers song that hasn't been popular in at least ten years.

Together, we watch as Leo, the driver, sets his phone on top of a pile of boxes before breaking into a well-choreographed dance while still standing in the back of the truck. Leo hoists his hands up over his head, swaying them back and forth while grape-vining back and forth in the small space. He sings along to the music, thrusting his hips in an overly dramatic and nearly comical gyration before ending his routine with a spin and a wink to the camera.

Aiden and I break into applause, catching Leo off guard. He momentarily startles before breaking into a grin. Hopping down from the back of the truck, he does a little dance over to where we sit at the table. "Didn't know I had an audience!"

"Breaking hearts all over the world with more of those dances?" I ask, pointing to the phone in his hand.

He gives me a salacious grin while shamelessly flexing his biceps. "You know how it is—just out here doing the Lord's work."

"How many followers do you even have, man?" Aiden asks.

"Ah, I just hit fifty-three thousand on TikTok, and I'm holding steady at a little over fifteen thousand on Instagram."

"Holy fuck, dude. All from short videos of you acting like a fucking fool? Maybe I should start dancing for High Tide."

I laugh along with Leo, who takes no offense to Aiden, but the idea does ignite something in my mind. "Maybe we start with an Instagram presence and focus on creative ways to showcase our products that are specific to this location—something different than the corporate account. Would you want to be in charge of that account for the store? I've seen a few pictures of what you've posted on your own account, and you're really good with photography."

Aiden looks excited at the prospect, and in turn, it excites me.

Giving him something to focus on, handing him something to be proud of creating and curating, could be a great way to really get him to flourish. And a small part of my decision gives me hope that he'll continue to learn that I am here for him as more than just a boss but as a friend, too.

And while I'm not ready to give up on the conversation we started before Leo pulled up, both Aiden and I stand and help carry several boxes into the store, leaving the unspoken words for another time.

Seventeen

Luna Sea Plaza
Owner's Chat

CAMPBELL: Is there a stoner convention happening at High Tide today?

CAMPBELL: I swear the smell is permeating into the fabric of the stuffed animals in my shop.

ESME: Well, it's 420, so if there were a stoner convention, it would surely be held today.

CAMPBELL: Absolutely unacceptable.

CAMPBELL: The odor is nauseating.

SUNDAY: Don't fear the reefer.

ESME: Keep calm and get medicated.

ESME: Maybe a little bit of THC would help you chill out.

CAMPBELL: Never going to happen. I don't do drugs.

ESME: It's not a drug. It's a plant.

HOLLIS: Yeah, don't panic, Campbell. It's organic.

SUNDAY: And gluten-free!

MAEVE: Sorry for the bluntness, but you know by now that's just how we roll.

IMOGEN: *GIF of old woman saying I feel like I don't really care*

WATSON: It's one day. Give them a break.

WATSON: Besides, good buds have to stick together.

MAEVE: Watson! *Laughing emoji*

OAKEN: Hey! You finally got a new phone!

WATSON: Was sick of nearly slicing off my fingerprints on the cracked screen.

OAKEN: About time!

CAMPBELL: I'll let it go for today.

CAMPBELL: But if I have to replace inventory, I will be holding you responsible.

ESME: Aw, Campbell. Weed go well together if you'd simply give us all a chance.

SUNDAY: Yes, girl!

SUNDAY: God, I love having you here!

IMOGEN: *GIF people banging on table chanting one of us*

Eighteen
Imogen

WITH THE START OF SUMMER QUICKLY CREEPING UP ON US, LUNA Harbor has begun to see an almost daily influx of tourists from out of state. And while we locals love to spend as much time at the beach as possible, we also love to help keep our community clean, all the while laughing and having fun.

Even before The Grateful Thread opened, I was an active member in organizing volunteers to help with beach clean-up efforts and once I began to make friends with other people around the plaza, I knew it would be a great way to give back while still spending time with some of the people I cared about most.

And now, on the last weekend of May, I have Esme, Ezra, and Zander along with my normal crew of Luna Sea Plaza employees.

We don matching reflective vests that are the very opposite of fashion forward, and as we walk the shoreline, weaving in and out of sunbathers with oversized colorful umbrellas, we collect trash both left behind by beachgoers as well as treasures washed ashore from worlds away. Using trash pickers—the kind Grandma Birdie keeps in her kitchen to grab mugs off the top shelf—we collect everything from cigarette butts to empty potato chip bags.

Sunny and her daughter run ahead, the five-year-old running closer to the water before giggling and running back to dry sand each time a wave crashes along the shore.

It's bright and sunny, breezy and hot without being oppressive, and while I'm sweating under my safety vest, I'm happy—despite having just picked up a used diaper buried under a pile of sand.

Holding up a flip-flop between his garbage picker's tongs, Zander waves it in the air. "This counts for the contest!"

Watson, the elderly owner of Sure Lock Homes, laughs. "Son, you'll find enough flip-flops before the day is finished to open up your own shoe store." Struggling through the sand that sinks with each step, he takes a seat at the base of a nearby lifeguard stand. In his late sixties, Watson has been having an increasingly difficult time maneuvering life after a near-fatal car accident nearly two years ago. But aside from his time in the hospital and rehabilitation center, he's refused to miss a plaza-wide beach cleanup. "It's the most out-of-place item you're looking for. Think of things you would never expect to find on a beach."

"I've got a toothbrush!" Hollis hollers.

"That's more like it!" Watson responds.

I take a seat next to Watson, thankful for the brief reprieve after what has been several hours of combing the shoreline. He gives me a grandfatherly pat on the knee. "If it's alright with you, dear, I think I'm going to stay here while you younglings finish up and dispose of the trash. I'll start on getting everything set up for the bonfire—as soon as my old hips will allow me to stand again."

With every beach cleanup we do, we cap off the night with a bonfire complete with hot dogs, s'mores, music, and laughter. It's become a tradition of sorts, a way to pat ourselves on the back for a job well done, while celebrating the successes of everyone from Luna Sea Plaza.

As the sun begins its nightly routine of turning in for the night, we all reconvene near the lifeguard tower. Our own night is just about to begin as most of the tourists leave the sand to head back to their hotel rooms, where they will undoubtedly slather handfuls of aloe over sun-kissed skin. Those of us who already spent the day on the beach are joined by our fellow employees, friends, and family, who bring armfuls of provisions for the night.

Oaken pulls a cooler behind him, struggling to maneuver the case over the sand as he does almost every time he joins us for a post-cleanup fire. Taking note, Zander scurries to where he is coming from, pushing from behind as the wheels continue to sink into the powdery sand.

Just as he said he would, Watson has amassed a large pile of wood, stacking it neatly into a large, deep hole he dug in the sand. We set up folding beach chairs around where the fire will be started, and thanks to Maeve and her husband, we even have a folding table to keep our food up and away from as much sand as possible.

Grandma Birdie arrives with Eileen, the older woman who works at High Tide, and soon after, Allison, Aveline, and Aiden arrive, too.

"It's the Triple-A Team!" Sunday calls out upon their arrival.

My parents stop by, a guitar case in my father's hand. And when he sits down and begins to pluck the strings, I'm transported back to the summers of my youth where he would spend hours entertaining our family at bonfires much like this.

Watson lights the fire as the majority of everyone starts to settle down in chairs, while several people, myself included, choose to sit on towels right on the sand. Long, metal skewers are passed out for hog dogs, and as we roast our dinner over open flame, we softly sing along to *Wagon Wheel* before my dad transitions into a medley of Grateful Dead songs known by only a few of the people around the fire.

Across the flames, I watch as Esme stands from her chair before she moves to a cooler, two cold beers in hand. Instead of returning to her seat, she crosses to me, holding out one of the glass bottles with the top already removed. Gratefully, I accept the beverage and pat the ground next to me, urging her to take a seat.

Without hesitation, I nuzzle into the warmth of her body, and although the fire burns in the now-dark sky just feet away from us, she's warmer than the roaring flames could ever be. My head rests gently on her shoulder, a smile softly playing on my lips.

Esme turns her head, placing a small kiss to the crown of my own. "This night is fucking magical, isn't it?"

"Mmm, it really is."

"Reminds me of nights when we used to sneak shitty wine coolers from your parents' fridge and sneak out here to watch the stars."

"Oh, my God, I totally forgot about that!" I laugh. "Remember the time we tried that peach tropical punch? Christ, that drink was awful."

Now, it's Esme's turn to laugh. "It really was. No wonder it was discontinued."

My mom laughs from her spot still next to my father. "You both think we didn't know you were sneaking out with provisions from the fridge? Hell, after a while we just started buying the grossest things we could get our hands on just to watch it disappear."

Everyone bursts out into laughter, while Esme and I simply shake our heads in disbelief.

Esme has seen my parents a few times since she came back just a few short months ago. The day I arrived for dinner with her in tow—not telling my parents she was in Luna Harbor—was one of the most emotional days of my life. My mother gasped, pulling her into a deep hug. As the two pulled apart from one another, my mom held her at arm's length while tears spilled from both of their eyes. We laughed and recounted stories of our youth, often hearing my parents' point of view for the first time.

Apparently, according to my mom and dad, the two of us

together have always been known troublemakers—even if we thought we were always sweet as pie.

I continue to watch the fire dance in front of us, music still continuing to play from the acoustic guitar met by the natural music of crashing waves. Sunday helps her daughter roast a marshmallow, Birdie and Eileen discuss the best vacations they've ever taken, and Hollis and Maeve bounce ideas off each other for the upcoming Luna Sea Lunacy party that's just a few weeks away, while Maeve's husband, Sebastian, sits closely by her side.

Asher joins us, playfully tossing a football into the air, and it isn't long before he has a few people organized for a game. Under the moonlight, they split into teams, and when the teams are uneven, Esme volunteers to play. She gives me a small smile and the quickest of kisses against my lips before scurrying away, her long legs on display in small shorts.

Although she just left my side, I miss her warmth.

Since she treated me to our first date, I have found myself becoming increasingly infatuated with the woman. But in all honesty, I think it's simply that those strong feelings never fully dissipated to begin with. She was always my person, my world. Now that she's back in my orbit, I never want her to leave again.

Some people may call it codependency, but I know it's knowing you're meant to be with someone and wanting to spend every moment with them. Being content to be near, even if you're not speaking, but just wanting to exist in the same space as the person who brings you joy and light.

And while Esme has promised that she is here for good, that she will never leave my side again, I still have a niggle of doubt that one day, I'll wake up, and she'll be gone.

Birdie plops down in the sand next to where I'm sitting. "You're going to have to help me up after this." I lean my head on her shoulder, much like I previously did with Esme. My grandmother has always been my rock, and like the dirty, little mind reader that she is, she always knows when my mind is swirling, sometimes, even before I truly know it for myself. "What's going on, peanut? You look like you're deep in thought over here."

I give a little shrug in response, but my grandmother doesn't buy it.

"When I first met your grandfather, I was as the kids say, a smitten kitten. He had this almost sandy-blonde hair and bright, blue eyes that crinkled around the corners when he laughed. We had met at church, which was common for the time, and soon began spending all our time together. We were young and dumb, but God, did we love each other; we did until the day he took his last breath."

I can't see my grandmother's face, but I wouldn't be surprised if there were tears in her eyes.

"Over the years, we grew together. We had three beautiful children together, cheered for each other when we reached goals, and mourned with one another when one of us was hurting. I expected forever, but one careless decision from an irresponsible person took him away from me. It kills me to this day that he never had the chance to meet you or your sister. He would have simply adored you. Still, my sweet girl, through all the pain and longing, through feeling like I didn't show him enough each and every day how much I loved him, I wouldn't have it any other way because I was able to have him in my life for nearly four decades. Sometimes, you need to take the risk and love those people in your life—no matter how long that time ends up lasting."

Her voice breaks on the last few words and it causes a surge of emotion inside me, making my chest feel heavy.

I watch Esme on the other side of the fire, still playfully tossing and catching a football with so many of the people I love. And at that moment, I decide that Grandma Birdie is right. No matter how long we have together, it's time that I start to show her exactly what she means to me.

Pushing up from the sand, I hold a hand out to my grandmother next, but she politely declines, insisting she wants to stay where it is nice and toasty for just a bit longer.

I weave my way through my friends, finding Esme quickly. I pull her away from the crowd and into my arms, pressing her lips to mine without a care for who might see.

"Hey there, gorgeous." She kisses me on the lips again before dropping another kiss to the crown of my head. Those little gestures, the innocent kisses and hand squeezes cut straight through to my core; they always have. "I could get used to a greeting like this."

Still in her arms, I dig deep and find the confidence I need to move forward, knowing that whatever happens between Esme and me in the long run has already been determined by fate—maybe long before either of us were even a blip in the universe. Pushing up on my tip toes, I close the few inches between her ear and my lips and whisper into the night, "Instead of greetings, let's say goodnight to everyone."

"Ready to leave already?"

I look at her with incredulity, surprised she didn't get my hint. Trying again, this time, I say, "I'm ready for *you* to take *me* home."

Esme stills, her eyes searching mine with a new intensity I haven't seen before. It's as if her usual chocolate-brown eyes have transformed into deep, dark pools of obsidian, like she finally grasps the meaning of my insinuation. "Lead the way, sweet girl."

Nineteen
Luna Sea Plaza
Owner's Chat

SUNDAY: Imogen and Esme sitting in a tree...

HOLLIS: K-I-S-S-I-N-G!

MAEVE: You guys got out of here faster than someone running from the cops!

HOLLIS: I seriously hope you're getting the banging of your life right now.

MAEVE: Getting slammed like a screen door in a summer storm!

OAKEN: Brown chicken brown cow!

HOLLIS: What the actual fuck?

OAKEN: ...

MAEVE: Do you mean "bow chicka wow wow?"

OAKEN: Well, that makes significantly more sense.

SUNDAY: Oh. My. God.

HOLLIS: I can't...I can't stop laughing.

OAKEN: Oh, shut it, Mistress of the Dark and Debauched.

MAEVE: *Laughing emoji* *Laughing emoji* *Laughing emoji*

MAEVE: Actual tears are leaking from my eyes right now.

SUNDAY: Oh, I kinda love that nickname for you, Hollis!

HOLLIS: Keep it up, big guy. I've got a ball gag that would look lovely between those full lips of yours.

OAKEN: Fuckkkkkkk...

Twenty
Esme

On a normal day, it takes approximately twelve minutes to make it from the public parking lot at the beach to my apartment. Tonight, I make it back to my small, peaceful space in eight. All the while, I sneak glances at Imogen as she sits next to me, quietly singing along to *Dancing Queen* as it plays on a loop.

I can't help but hold back a laugh as I pull the car into the driveway, thinking back to the startled look on her face the day she slid into the passenger seat trying—and failing—to turn the volume up.

"The Farleys' house?" Imogen asks when she sees where we are.

Giving her a nod, I open my own car door before circling to open hers. "They rented me the apartment over their garage. It's not much, but it works for me, and it's a place I can call mine."

Anita Farley, the older woman who owns the house along with her husband, was our school librarian and a woman completely ahead of her time. While most other schools were only beginning to include literature on tough subjects like race and gender, Mrs. Farley was cultivating a space of inclusion and education. Much to the dismay of several parents in our school district, she pushed to make sure everyone knew they were welcomed in her library, and when several books came under fire from local anti-inclusive groups, she complied with the school district's request to remove them from our middle school library but not before building a Little Free Library outside of her house, filling it with those very books and resources.

I hold out a hand to Imogen, who willingly accepts it. She steps out of the car with a practiced grace that envelopes all her movements, almost as if each step holds a carefully choreographed dance move designed specifically to drive me crazy.

We ascend the stairs to the apartment, Immy in front of me, my hand on the curve of her lower back. Reaching around her frame, I turn the lock in the keyhole and allow her to cross the threshold into my space.

She carefully studies the apartment, eyes traveling over the few decorations I've placed on a shelf that lines the corner of the living room. A small TV sits on a metal stand, an old IKEA piece I found sitting on the side of the road on trash night a few weeks back. Its teal color reminds me of the place where the ocean meets the sky on a clear day, and the intricate pattern across the two sliding doors on the front reminds me of something whimsical that would be found at Magical Mystical Mayhem. Of course, the inside shelves of mine contain a few books and movies, not the tarot cards and incense I imagine they would store inside of theirs.

Crossing to the bookshelf, she picks up a lone picture that sits in a silver frame, studying it with great intensity. When she turns back to me, I notice the unshed tears in her eyes.

"This is the first picture we ever took together," she says, a quake in her voice.

I take the picture from her hand and place it back on the shelf. We stare at it together, the two young girls with their heads pressed together, silly smiles on their faces, oversized bows in their hair, and so much adoration in their eyes. Even then, at the age of seven, I knew there was something extra special about Imogen. Even then, I knew she was the person I would spend my life with. I might not have understood what role she would play, but I knew she would be my constant.

"There might not be a lot I have from my life before I came back to you, but everything I have, I treasure every damn day."

A tear escapes, and I quickly reach out to wipe it from her cheek.

"Will you tell me what happened?" she asks, so quietly I almost don't hear her.

I give her an apologetic smile, not wanting to diminish the growing need that has been radiating between us since the moment she asked me to take her home. "One day soon, I promise."

Imogen opens her mouth as if to speak but closes it again before giving me a short nod. Finally, she replies, "When you're ready."

"Come on." I take her hand in mine. "I have something else I want to show you."

While the apartment is small, the bedroom has its own room, a tiny nook off to the right of the main living space that is just big enough to fit my queen-sized bed, dresser, and nightstand. Flicking on the light, I allow Imogen to pass into the room. She manages two steps before she stops in her tracks, a gasp echoing in the otherwise silent room.

Still holding her hand, we walk to my bed, but neither of us sit on top of the mattress. Imogen's free hand gently runs over the quilt that lays across my bed. The pinks and oranges have faded with time, but despite the faded colors, it's just as vibrant as the day it was made thanks to the love and memories between the fabric.

"It was my warmth every single day that I was away from you. I've cried tears of sadness into it, and I've smiled at the memories it has given me. And more than anything else, I prayed for the day when I would get to lay you down on top of it and claim you as mine again."

Leaning into her body, I capture her lips with mine in a near savage kiss. Imogen's body melts against mine, a hand coming up to tangle in the mess of curls that is my forever unruly hair. She meets me with reverent ministrations of her own lips as we nip and lick at one another like two parched souls finding a coveted oasis deep within a barren desert.

Pulling away, she keeps her forehead close enough to press against mine. "I never thought I'd see you again. Never thought that I'd be able to hold your hand or kiss you, never thought that I'd be able to feel your skin against mine. You're everything to me, Esme. *Everything*."

"And you're everything to me, baby. Always have been, always will."

I kiss her once more, slowly pushing her backward until her thighs meet the mattress. Sitting on top of our memories, I continue to push gently against her chest. When her back meets the quilt, I take a second to take in the most beautiful sight I've ever seen.

Still in a lilac sundress that she wore throughout the beach clean-up and bonfire, I can just about make out the outline of her flimsy swimsuit underneath the fabric. Her nipples are peaked and pebbled, straining against both layers as if in a silent plea for my lips to wrap around them. Her hair has transformed over the last few weeks, from a deep, rich brown to a slightly lighter caramel that has been naturally highlighted from the sun. It splays out around her like a halo, and my fingers itch to reach out and wrap it around my fingers.

I crawl over her body, pressing one of my thighs between hers, which she willingly spreads wider. Imogen arches her back when I slide my leg against her fabric covered sex, and as a groan spills from her lips, I capture the sound with my mouth, wanting every sound she makes to be mine.

Giving into the urge, I tangle my fingers into her hair, lightly tugging her head to the side before devouring the salt-kissed skin of her neck. Kiss after kiss, I press my lips against her skin, alternating between gentle bites and small sucks, between licks and chaste kisses that leave her breathless.

As I hold myself over her body with one hand, the other trails down her neck, over the gentle slope of her collarbone, until I'm cupping her breast. Imogen presses her body closer to mine, moaning as my lips follow the same pathway my hand just traversed.

I take her nipple into my mouth, biting over the fabric of her bathing suit and dress while palming her other breast. Her soft gasps and moans spur me on, audibly confirming that she is just as needy for me as I am for her.

Wanting to prolong the noises echoing in the otherwise silent room, I tease her more over her clothes, running my hands up and down her body, lightly scraping my nails against her bare arms. I push the hem of her skirt up around her hips, needing to feel more bare skin under my fingertips. Without words, Imogen pushes herself up long enough to pull the fabric over her head, discarding it next to us on the mattress.

Her own hands, soft and delicate, roam over my body, pushing up the hem of my shirt and skimming over the bare skin of my stomach. She drags her short nails over my skin in tantalizing strokes, alternating the movements with soft caresses. All the while, I stare at the now almost-naked woman beneath me.

Imogen's breasts spill from the cups of her swimsuit, the slightly dusky color of her nipples cresting over the contrasting black fabric. I take a moment to revel in her curves—the gentle hourglass figure of her hips and thick thighs that I can't wait to get lost between.

Reaching down, I pull the cups of her suit lower, fully freeing her tits, and I swear to God, my mouth fucking waters. I capture one perfect nipple between my lips, teasing her with gentle suction and slow, lazy caresses of my tongue.

Moving lower, I continue to pepper her bare skin with kisses, loving the way goosebumps spread across her skin in my wake.

Imogen giggles when my tongue dips into the shallow pool of her belly button, pants when I nip at the soft flesh of her stomach, and moans when I push her thighs further apart, placing a kiss on top of the fabric still covering the one place I'm desperate for.

A wet spot has formed between her thighs, barely visible on the dark fabric of her suit bottoms, but there nonetheless, teasing me and tempting me to brush my lips over the one place of Imogen's body that I've never tasted before.

"I need to get my mouth on you, sweetheart."

Imogen lifts her hips in response, urging me to slide her bottoms over her ass, down her thighs, and around her calves. I hold onto her legs, staring at her center, already glistening with arousal. Shaved bare, her skin is smooth, and I catch sight of a birthmark that I never noticed before.

Then again, in all our other times together, we were young and timid. Inexperienced and apprehensive as we explored the feelings we shared along with the newness of sharing our bodies, too.

But now, we're no longer scared teenagers. We're women with vastly different bodies than we had ten years ago.

I love this version of Imogen even more.

Gliding my hands up her legs, I follow their path with kisses. The sole of her foot, her ankle, several up the smooth expanse of her calf.

"God, I could come just from you touching me," she moans as I place a kiss behind her knee.

I nip her with my teeth on the next kiss, causing her to squeal. "Don't you fucking dare, Imogen." My voice comes out stern and deeper than usual, almost as if I'm subconsciously angry that she would even joke about not allowing me to bring her fully to orgasm in the one way I so desperately want.

She whines as I place another kiss, this time at the juncture of her thigh. Redness mars the beautiful skin between her thighs, no doubt the result of hours combing the beach in a sundress, yet she's no less beautiful for it. If anything, seeing her so true to life is intoxicating. "Then stop teasing me."

"For ten years, I've been dreaming about this moment. I'm going to savor this. Savor your skin, and your moans, and the taste of your sweet pussy."

While still kissing her skin, I grip her hip with one hand, dipping the other between her legs. I trail the very tips of my fingers over her body, teasing her labia but never delving deeper to the place she is all but begging for me to touch.

"Esme, please!" It's a plea—a needy little mewl.

I drape one of her legs lazily over my shoulder. "You were a beautiful girl, sweetheart." Repeating the process, I rest her other leg over my opposite shoulder. "You're now an even a more beautiful woman." I lower my head to her center, inhaling the scent of arousal and sweat with a hint of the salty tang of the ocean's water. It's a heady combination, one I'm too eager to get lost in. "But fuck, baby, you're bossy as hell."

Finally, my lips connect with her sweet pussy. I part Imogen's folds with my fingers, licking her from opening to clit with one long and fluid movement.

I want to go slow, to savor this moment for every second it lasts, but when my tongue connects with her cunt and I finally get a taste of her sweet pussy, I all but lose control. Over and over again, I lick against her skin, luxuriating in the flavor of Imogen as she slides against my tongue. I suck on her clit before gently biting her most sensitive place, eliciting a delicious moan from the woman spread wide for me.

"You feel *so* good," she tells me.

"Not as good as you taste, sweetheart."

Sliding two fingers deep inside, I continue to assault her with my tongue as well, alternating between languorous licks and quick nips, soft kisses and rough suction.

My saliva pools around us, her pussy even wetter from the

mixture of her arousal and my spit. It slides from between her lips and runs between her ass cheeks, covering the delicate rosebud of her ass.

While keeping up the pace with my fingers, I lower my head further, giving one flat swipe of my tongue over the sensitive hole. She bucks against me, her muscles clenching on the fingers deep inside her cunt.

One, two, three more licks and I return to my previous position, lips wrapped around her now-throbbing clit. I dart out my tongue, flicking against the bundle of sensitive nerve endings as she screams into my bedroom, coming apart under the combination of fingers and tongue.

Imogen's hands reach out to me, firmly grabbing my curls between her fingers. She grinds against my face, chasing every last ounce of pleasure. And I let her, wanting to be the reason her skin is coated with such a glorious sheen, the reason why her voice has gone hoarse as she chants my name.

I crawl up her body, pulling her into my arms and placing sweet kisses upon her lips. She says my name again—a quiet little prayer. And if I have anything to say about it, my name will be the only name she ever yells or whispers into the silent confines of a room again.

Twenty-One

Luna Sea Plaza
Owner's Chat

MAEVE: Last minute meeting for the parking lot party tonight at 6:30.

> IMOGEN: Need us to host? We don't have any classes tonight.

MAEVE: Nah, I've got space in the event room at the bookshop.

ESME: I can bring a few snacks.

CAMPBELL: If there are any type of mind-altering substances being ingested at this meeting, you can kindly count me out.

SUNDAY: You should really rename your store to Cranky Campbell's Timeless Toys.

HOLLIS: That tracks.

> IMOGEN: *GIF of woman spitting out water*

WATSON: TRACKS? ARE WE HUNTING SMALL ANIMALS?

HOLLIS: It's slang.

WATSON: FOR WHAT?

HOLLIS: It's true.

WATSON: WHAT'S TRUE?

HOLLIS: That tracks.

WATSON: I ALREADY ASKED YOU. TRACKS WHAT?

SUNDAY: That tracks is slang for it's true.

WATSON: NOW WAS THAT SO HARD TO EXPLAIN?

MAEVE: Christ on a cracker.

IMOGEN: *GIF of Michael Scott laughing*

WATSON: I WILL BE THERE.

OAKEN: No need to shout, old man.

WATSON: I'M NOT SHOUTING. I DO NOT KNOW HOW TO TURN OFF CAPS LOCK ON THIS BLASTED DEVICE.

WATSON: GOING TO CALL MY GRANDSON ABOUT THIS.

WATSON: SEE YOU AT 6:30.

CAMPBELL: If there is nothing else to discuss, I will see you all at 6:30 this evening.

Luna Sea Plaza Owner's Chat

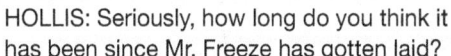

HOLLIS: Seriously, how long do you think it has been since Mr. Freeze has gotten laid?

MAEVE: He's even more insufferable lately.

> IMOGEN: *GIF of Frozone from The Incredibles*

> IMOGEN: You guys, can I PLEASE invite Esme into this chat now?

OAKEN: Fine by me.

MAEVE: I second the movement.

SUNDAY: I haven't been the holdout this entire time.

HOLLIS: Hey! I'm just protective of this space!

HOLLIS: But yeah, it's been a few months now. Add her to the chat.

> IMOGEN: *GIF of child beauty pageant kid twerking*

Esme has been added to the Luna Sea Plaza COOL Owner's Chat

> IMOGEN: Hey, beautiful. Welcome to the actual party!

OAKEN: I'm totally down for special snacks for tonight's meeting if you are.

ESME: What the hell! You've all been holding out on me!

> IMOGEN: *GIF of chirping crickets*

SUNDAY: The first rule of the Luna Sea Plaza COOL Owner's Chat is that we don't talk about the Luna Sea Plaza COOL Owner's Chat.

ESME: I have no idea what you're talking about.

HOLLIS: The second rule is whatever happens in this chat, stays in this chat. No screenshots.

MAEVE: Because screenshots are forever!

ESME: Noted.

> IMOGEN: *GIF of Christian Grey saying good girl*

ESME: Nah, baby. That's all you.

SUNDAY: Oh. Hell. Yes.

MAEVE: I shouldn't be turned on by that, yet here I am.

OAKEN: ...same?

HOLLIS: It's natural to be turned on by observing the sexual exploits of others. Look up voyeurism if you don't believe me.

HOLLIS: Or just talk to Maeve.

> IMOGEN: *GIF of woman blushing*

> IMOGEN: *GIF of a woman fainting*

> IMOGEN: I hate you all.

ESME: You love me, and you know it. See you all in a few hours!

Twenty-Two
Imogen

IT'S A RARITY TO GET ALL THE SHOP OWNERS FROM LUNA SEA Plaza in one location, something that happens maybe twice a year, at most. But with Luna Sea Lunacy just a few days away, it truly is all-hands-on deck around the plaza.

I stroll into the event space at Black, White, and Read all over, taking a seat next to Esme who is already talking with Maeve. Hollis and Watson are also already in the room, and Maeve lets us know we'll begin in just a few minutes.

Dropping a quick kiss to Esme's cheek, she turns from Maeve to give me a huge, goofy grin, her adorable dimples popping in the corner of her cheeks.

"I have a bone to pick with you," I tell her.

Esme's body tenses in her chair, and I hurry to speak again, not wanting her to think that I actually have something bad to tell her. I've noticed her do the same thing several times in the last few months, and I internally remind myself to try and approach her with more caution in the future. I never want her to think I'm angry at her, especially without reason. "Did you give my grandmother the shirt she has on today?"

She gives me a confused look, her brows scrunching in the middle to create the cutest little crease. "No, I haven't given her any shirts."

Pulling my phone from the pocket of my dress, I swipe open the photos app before sliding it in front of Esme. A quick glance at the photo sends her into raucous laughter.

She slides the phone across the table to Hollis, who repeats the process, showing the phone screen to Maeve.

"What? I don't get to see?" Watson asks, no doubt feeling left out of the fun.

He takes a turn, looking at the phone screen before breaking out into laughter. "That Birdie is something else," he says with another chuckle.

"You're telling me not all grandmothers in their late seventies parade around town wearing a shirt with a giraffe on it that reads *higher than a giraffe's vagina*?"

Campbell takes that moment to enter the room, shooting disapproving glances at those of us who have already gathered. A few minutes later, the two remaining shop owners join us, and we begin going over plans for the day of our plaza-wide party.

"I have a few vendors who will be dropping off food trucks the night before," Maeve says. "I'll be out in the lot that evening, instructing everyone where to park. Permits have all been acquired by the city, and we are good to have customers park in the open field across the street again this year. Signage should be delivered tomorrow afternoon."

She continues, filling us in on everything that has been happening behind the scenes over the last few weeks, and I thank God that it's Maeve heading up the event. This party has about a million and one different moving parts, none of which I have any desire to be in charge of. "The Facebook event has really picked up over the last week with over two thousand replies, and I really think that is in part to all of you who have been passing out flyers to your customers."

Campbell speaks up. "We had flyers to pass out?"

Maeve's glare could revert climate change with how icily she stares at him.

"Maybe if you actually participated a bit more around here, you would know that there have been flyers for weeks," Sunday quips from her seat next to Oaken.

"It was in the owner group chat a few weeks ago, as well as in the email I sent out to all the stores about the event. I instructed everyone to come by to pick up a stack and to let me know when each store ran out," Maeve tells Campbell.

He huffs in exasperation. "Group chat, email threads, smoke signals. Next you'll be sending me a fucking fax. I just want to run my shop and go home at the end of my day. I can't be bothered with all this other shit all the time!"

"Nobody uses faxes anymore," Oaken tells him in a huff of his own.

Personally, I love all the communication between everyone in the plaza. It feels like so much more than a job when you're able to create a strong bond with the people you see on a near-daily basis. The group chats, the almost daily stops we make in each other's businesses—it's turned from simply owning a store at Luna Sea Plaza to feeling like almost all these people are friends, like they're part of my extended family.

But on the other hand, I *totally* can't wait to see what the cool owner's chat has to say about Campbell's little outburst later tonight. Thank the heavens for a space where we can talk without him being a constant rain cloud hovering over our fun.

We spend close to another hour talking about logistics—the timeline for the day, the vendors who will be joining us, the entertainment scheduled for throughout the day. The longer we talk, the more excited I get for the parking lot party.

As we end the meeting, I kiss Esme again before rising from my seat, ready to return to The Grateful Thread to finish up the rest of my evening shift. Esme attempts to follow but is corralled by Hollis. I hold up my phone, mouthing the words *text me* before blowing her a kiss and slipping from the event space at the bookshop.

With the meeting running slightly over time, it's less than an hour until we lock up for the night. I send Birdie home, giraffe vagina shirt and all, and tell her I'll be fine taking care of our end of night tasks on my own. She loves the parking lot party as much as the rest of us, and with her age, I want to be sure she is well rested and able to fully participate in as much of the upcoming day as she can.

After the clock ticks past closing time, I switch off the neon open sign—complete with a spool of thread and a needle all in bright, fluorescent colors—and flip the lock on the front door. I make a quick sweep around the store, straightening up fabric and accessories. Tonight, the *sewing, because murder is wrong* sign is crooked, and like I do almost nightly, I take a second to straighten it out along with any others that were knocked off kilter during the day.

As I'm sitting behind the front desk, working on balancing our drawer for the evening, I hear a knock at the glass door and glance up from my work to find Esme. With High Tide closing an hour later than we do, it isn't unusual for her to swing by to say goodnight before I leave for the evening, and it always leaves me with a smile on my face.

Opening the door, I usher her into the dimly lit shop. Barely giving me enough time to engage the lock again, she has me turned around, back against the glass windows that line the front of the store.

"What are you doing?" I ask, slightly out of breath from the unexpected onslaught of kisses.

"Are you the only one here?" she asks, her voice rolling over my skin like smooth silk.

A nod is the only response I muster before she is dragging me by the hand toward the back of the shop. Esme pushes open the door to our small storage room, dragging me in behind her. Lips on mine again, she speaks through even more kisses while walking backward to a low, built in cabinet. "You saw Hollis pull me aside at the end of the meeting?"

"Yes." I'm near breathless in my reply.

"She said she had something she thought I might enjoy. That

we might enjoy." Esme rolls her hips into me, and I immediately feel the difference. Where we normally fit flush against each other, now there is something hard and impressively long under the fabric of her clothes. "Let me make you feel good, sweetheart."

"He…here?"

"Yeah, baby. Here." She slides one hand down my torso before bunching up the fabric of my dress, caressing me over my panties. At the moment, I'm not sure if she means *here* as in the storage room or *here* as in between my thighs, but whatever it is she has in mind, I'll certainly be a willing participant.

We've been together more times than I can count since the night of the bonfire. And while we've explored each other's bodies with renewed vigor—with fingers and lips and tongues—we've yet to add toys into the mix.

Apparently, that's about to change.

I lean into her for a kiss, lightly tugging on her bottom lip before releasing it. Esme's arms circle around me before she lifts me up, placing me on the countertop. Her body is all lean and lithe, yet Esme is deceptively strong. She pulls back to look at me, and I widen my thighs in a silent answer while pushing soft fabric and shiny spools of ribbon from the counter around me. "Do it," I tell her. "Make me feel good."

I slide my dress up my body, shimmying it over my head until I'm left in nothing but a simple nude bra and cotton panties —a far cry from the colorful clothing I generally wear. Running my own palms over my body, I let one still on my breast while the other travels further down, coming to rest on my cotton-clad cunt. Giving her a slow smile, I'm already half-drunk on the combination of how badly she wants me and how extremely turned on she can make me with nothing but simple words. I pull my panties to the side, gliding one finger through my center. Esme watches with rapt attention, her eyes never straying from the gentle strokes I give myself. "Make me feel good here."

She captures my wrist in her hand before I can slide my fingers deep inside myself. Stilling my movements before lifting my hand to her mouth, her pink tongue darts out between her equally pink lips, licking along the length of my fingers to taste the remnants of my arousal. "I'll always make you feel good, sweetheart. I'm greedy for you—greedy to make you feel good. I want all your orgasms, all your screams and moans."

Esme pulls at the button of her jeans before sliding the zipper down. "Fuck, baby, I'm jealous of anyone else who has ever touched you. I'm jealous of your fingers because they've been able to touch your body every day that I wasn't there to do it for you."

With one fluid motion, she pushes down her jeans and panties, a large, purple silicone toy jutting out from between her legs. There are no straps, no harness holding it to her body and despite the color, it's extremely lifelike with a thick, mushroomed head and wide veins running down its length.

I must stare in awe, finally getting distracted when Esme spits into her hand and runs it over the toy in several rough strokes. She takes a step closer, and it's only then I can tell that the toy is nestled somewhere inside her body. "You wet enough to take me, baby?"

Heat pools deep in my belly at her dirty mouth, and if I wasn't already wet enough for her before she said those sinfully sexy words, I certainly am now.

I tug at the hem of her shirt, helping her to slide it over her head while she positions herself at my opening. Nudging the toy between my legs, Esme runs it up and down the length of my heat, slicking it through my wetness. Up and down, up and down, she rubs against me, never sliding into me and never quite reaching my clit in the cruelest of teases ever known.

Something between a huff and a moan falls from my lips at her next pass, the desperation coursing through my body close to a tipping point. Part of me wants to cry out in frustration, while the other part of me wants to demand that she stop teasing me and fuck me deep and hard.

"Tell me what you need, sweetheart. Tell me what that greedy little pussy of yours needs, and I'll give it to you."

"You," I all but pant. "I need you inside me. Need you to make me feel good."

Esme slides through me once again, but this time, she doesn't tease. Slowly, she pushes the toy into me, a delicious stretch overtaking my body as she moves in and out, a little deeper each time. While I've never been a huge fan of penetrative sex in the past, with Esme, it feels good. It feels right to have her inside me in such an intimate way.

I relish the feeling of the fake cock buried deep inside me, gasping as the stretch fades from a slight discomfort and blooms into an insurmountable pleasure.

Fully seated inside me, she leans over my body, pressing a soft kiss against my lips. "You good?"

"So good," I say as I pull the cups of Esme's bra down, desperate to get my hands on her gorgeous tits that fit perfectly in my palms.

Esme moans as I squeeze one of her nipples, rolling it between the pads of my fingers. "It's about to get even better."

With that, she reaches down between us, brushing against my clit with the lightest of movements before fumbling for a second at the place where the toy meets her body. She does something out of sight, and then the toy comes to life, vibrating around both of us as a gentle whirring noise fills the small, crowded storage room.

My eyes shut as the sensation runs through my body, but Esme's firm voice has me fulfilling her every command. "Open up, baby. Watch as I fuck your perfect pussy. Watch as I show you just how good we are together."

Not that I could ever doubt that we're good together.

Actually, fuck good. We're *perfect* together. Two puzzle

pieces meant to snap tightly into place, each curve perfectly situated to hold and hug those around it.

She holds my calves, one in each hand, nearly folding me in on myself as my back rests firmly against the wall behind me. Slowly, Esme begins to move again, sliding in and out while allowing me to become accustomed to the feel of the vibration.

Soon, my hips are meeting hers with each thrust, my ass coming up off the counter with each movement. Faster and faster, Esme pumps into me, and the sounds of our moans and gasps overtake the sounds of the vibration.

Changing the angle of her hips, Esme hits an entirely different place deep inside of me, and it's enough to send me over the edge. I gush around the toy, not even caring that I'm going to have to clean and disinfect everything before I can go home. My vision grows hazy around the edges, both light and darkness threatening to take over. A slick layer of sweat covers my skin as I squeeze my eyes shut. But they fly open when a quick but sturdy smack lands on the inside of my thigh. "Don't you dare shut those gorgeous, green eyes."

I watch Esme as she thrusts a few more times before she is moaning, body shaking with the force of her own orgasm. Still inside me, she lets my legs fall, allowing blood to begin flowing to my lower limbs again before reaching down to quiet the vibrations still teasing both of us.

We stay connected, both of us fighting for breath, as the aftershocks of pleasure tumble through our bodies. And though the toy isn't real, isn't an actual extension of Esme, I immediately miss the feel of it between my legs when she finally pulls out.

In silence, Esme helps me back into my dress before pulling her pants back up her legs and slipping her shirt over her head. I hop down from the counter, not at all gracefully. But nonetheless, Esme's lean arms are there, holding me steady as she so often does.

"Come over when you're done for the night?" I ask. "Stay the night with me?"

We've only had a few overnight visits in the last month, but I'm ready for more. I'm ready for all our nights to end in a tangle of limbs, while our mornings start in a tangle of linens. And there is only one person in the world I want to share that with.

Esme presses one last kiss to my lips before heading toward the storage room door. "Always, sweetheart. You want me in your bed, I'm sure as hell not going to say no."

We walk hand-and-hand through the store in a sex-mussed haze, and I unlock the front door for her to leave. I watch as she disappears down the sidewalk, back into High Tide with a smile on my face, knowing soon, she'll be walking through the door of my apartment.

Twenty-Three
Imogen

IMOGEN: You...

IMOGEN: Are...

IMOGEN: A...

IMOGEN: Goddess!

IMOGEN: Seriously, I'm not going to be able to walk straight for a week and I'm not one bit mad about it.

IMOGEN: I have no idea what that thing was, but holy shit was it AMAZING.

IMOGEN: Thanks for slipping it to Esme without me knowing.

HOLLIS: Ah, you like it?

IMOGEN: Do bears shit in the woods?

IMOGEN: Do ducks swim in circles?

IMOGEN: Is the pope Catholic?

HOLLIS: I'll be expecting a full review on my website at your earliest convenience.

IMOGEN: Sneaky little bitch!

HOLLIS: Thanks for being my product tester.
Wink emoji

IMOGEN: *GIF of woman saying happy to help*

Twenty-Four
Esme

WHILE THE HIGHLY ANTICIPATED PARKING LOT PARTY FOR OUR businesses is named *Luna Sea Lunacy*, I'm officially petitioning to rename it to *Simply Chaos*. Because as far as the eye can see this morning, that's exactly what is happening.

The clock hasn't even struck seven in the morning yet, but activity is bustling as vendors and store owners alike rush to set up for the party. Our normal parking lot, with space for just about one-hundred cars, is full of tents and canopies in various bright colors and patterns. Food vendors connect their trucks to generators, ready to gain power for the day, and I swear I can already smell the sweet scent of funnel cake wafting in the breeze.

A small stage is set up in the middle of the parking lot, several rows of folding chairs set in neat rows in front of it. I can't wait to see it full of patrons as they listen to the live music while their kids dance to the tunes, hopped up on way too much sugar and festival food.

Making my way across the parking lot, I shoot Imogen and Birdie a wave. The pair are hard at work, creating a beautiful sidewalk display of fabrics in prints equally as loud as both of their personalities. Upon reaching their storefront, I pull Imogen into a hug, wrapping my arms firmly around her body.

"Morning, beautiful," I whisper into her ear in a small, private moment meant for just the two of us.

Grandma Birdie brings another bolt of fabric outside, dropping it off on top of a folding table. Then, before Imogen and I have time to separate, she is standing next to us, wrapping her own arms around both of us as much as she can. "I can't begin to tell you how wonderful it is to have you both here like this. It's like I finally have my full family back because you, darling Esme, were always a part of my family."

The sentiment has an unknown emotion bubbling up in my chest, making it feel tight yet bubbly at the same time. "And you've both always been mine," I manage to squeak out before my throat threatens to close as I hold back tears.

I spend several minutes helping Imogen finish her display before looking back out to the parking lot. I'm just in time to see a truck pull into the space with a dunk tank being pulled on an old, flatbed trailer.

"Holy shit," I exclaim out loud. "This day really is going to be crazy, isn't it?"

Immy loops her arms around my neck, placing a quick kiss against my lips. "You have absolutely no idea. You're going to love it."

"Not as much as I love you, I bet."

As soon as the words leave my mouth, I tense, my body freezing in place. I squeeze my eyes shut tightly, hoping that for once, this is a dream that I'll wake up from at any moment.

Of course, I love Imogen. I have quite possibly loved her since the very first day I met her. But now, after all these years, she deserves to be told that over a beautiful, candlelit dinner or after a romantic moonlight walk on the beach. Not on a sidewalk while surrounded by random vendors setting up for a glorified sidewalk sale.

But I don't have a chance to open my eyes, to see if this is a dream or some horrible reality where I just admitted my love to the girl of my dreams in the most unromantic way possible, because Imogen's lips are on mine.

She kisses me with urgency, pressing her lips against mine

again and again. Against the corner of my mouth and over the place where my dimples pop from when I'm smiling. A kiss to my temple and my cheek, across my eyes, still firmly shut, and finally, on the very tip of my nose.

Imogen cups my face in her delicate hands, her thumbs gently running over the sensitive skin under my eyes.

"You have absolutely no idea how much I love you, Esme. How much I've dreamed of having you back in my life as an adult. As a friend, yes, but even more importantly as a lover. And I know you still feel like you need to make something up to me, that somehow you need to make up for lost time, but I promise you, that right here and now is exactly where I want to be."

I finally open my eyes, staring back into Immy's understanding, emerald eyes as she continues to hold my gaze, thumbs still sweeping over my skin. "You deserve so much more than me, Imogen. But I'll spend every day of the rest of my life trying to prove that I am worthy of your love for as long as you'll have me."

She hugs me again, my body flush against her. "My sweet Esme, when are you going to learn that you are exactly what I've always wanted, exactly what I've always deserved? I am worthy of your love in the same very way you are worthy of mine. I love what we have, what we're building together."

Unable to let go, I cling to her until someone clearing their throat pulls us from the moment.

"Sorry, boss," Zander says, sounding sincere. "We've got about an hour until people start showing up for the party. What's the game plan?"

I send him to the shop with my keys, promising to be there in just a minute. When he is finally out of sight, I turn back to Imogen, smiling widely at her beautiful face. "I don't deserve you," I tell her.

She gives me a slightly sad smile in response before pressing one last kiss to my lips. "You do, and one day, I'm going to make you understand that. Now, go get set up for the day. Your place after everything is finished for the night?"

We agree to meet up later, and I find myself already wishing the day was over. As I go to leave, Imogen lightly swats at my backside. "Esme."

I turn back toward her voice, loving the beautiful smile on her face that illuminates her eyes.

"I never stopped loving you," is all she says before she turns around, her dress covered in tiny spools of thread swirling around her knees as she walks back inside The Grateful Thread.

A smile spreads across my own face, my cheeks hurting from the strain as I stare off in the direction she went. Finally, I force myself to move to High Tide, knowing I need to be there for my team, no matter how distracted I am.

Zander gives me a sly smile, tossing my keys back to me as I enter the store. "You looked awfully cozy out there, boss," he says while wiggling his eyebrows suggestively.

"Oh, shut it, Z," I tell him. "One day, you'll fall in love and understand."

"Nah, there's no way. I'm never falling in love. Being with one woman for the rest of my life does not appeal to me in the slightest."

I can't help but roll my eyes. If he only knew how many times I've heard that in the past.

We open our doors to the public right at nine, and swear to God, the people don't stop flowing into the shop. All day long, our employees take turns enjoying the festivities outside while helping to pull orders and ring people up.

With the front door propped open, I can hear the music from the live band and smell the food as it wafts into the store. Looking at the large clock that hangs on the wall, I notice it's already past the afternoon hours and moving into early evening. No wonder my stomach is growling at me, begging for sustenance.

After checking with Aveline, I duck out to find something to stuff my face with. In search of deep-fried vegetables dunked in ranch dressing or potato pancakes slathered in sour cream, I scour the vendors and notice Maeve and Aiden cozying up to one another at a nearby picnic table that has been brought in for the occasion. She pulls off a piece of funnel cake from a plate, dragging it through a chocolate and hazelnut hazelnut sauce before feeding it to him. A bit of sauce catches on the side of his mouth, and as I watch from the hidden depths of the parking lot party, Maeve reaches out to swipe it away before sucking the sauce off her thumb. Aiden stares ahead as if in shock, while Maeve simply smiles at the young man. I follow her line of sight as she looks across the party and find her husband Sebastian leaning against a food truck. He watches the pair with rapt attention, his own eyes drifting between that of his wife and the young man she is sitting beside.

There is no malice in his gaze. No jealousy or fear. Instead, he looks almost hungry—and his hunger is certainly *not* for funnel cake.

Turning back to the task at hand, I find a food vendor and quickly pay for a hot dog, knowing that while I'm craving something fried, I shouldn't leave my staff alone for too long with how busy we've been all day.

I grab one of the folding chairs in front of the band, a local group playing covers that make me feel like I'm at some twisted version of *Lilith Fair*. My foot taps along as they sing their rendition of some one-hit-wonder song that I'm confident I haven't heard in at least five years.

With two bites left, I'm about to stand when movement in the chair to my right catches my attention. I turn to the person, expecting to see Imogen or one of the other regulars from around Luna Sea Plaza but am stunned silent at the face that greets me.

Long, blonde hair hangs in tight ringlets of curls down to her mid-back. She's wearing a simple pair of khaki shorts and a matching color top that make her look more like she is readying to embark on a safari trip as opposed to a day surrounded by the colorful cast of characters that make up the plaza. Lines crease her once smooth skin, and only now that I can focus on her presence do I notice the gray hair that has weaved itself through the golden curls.

"Esme." It's the only word she says as she studies me.

I want to push up from my chair and run back to the safety of my shop. Want to run to Imogen and cling to her body like a life raft. But I'm frozen in some combination of fear and shock, my ass unwilling to move from its spot in the metal folding chair.

Thinking if I close my eyes, she'll disappear, I slam them shut, squeezing my lids together until it's almost painful. Of course, when I open them, she's still there, not simply an unfortunate figment of my imagination.

Calling her mom doesn't sound right, neither does using her first name of Patricia. Instead, I look back to the band on stage, suddenly not hungry for the rest of my hot dog.

"You look well," she says after long, silent moments between us. "Healthy and happy."

I can't help the anger that is bubbling inside of my chest, lining my vision with red. I turn in my seat, fully facing her for the first time. My hands tightly balled into fists, I use the conscious pain of my short nails digging into my palms to fuel me through what I need to say.

"I am well," I tell her with a voice devoid of emotion. "I am healthy and happy, and that is through my own hard work and dedication. Not yours." She looks as if I've slapped her across the face, but I continue as the band shifts into its next song, a fitting rendition of *Foolish Games* played on the mandolin. "You and Dad made me feel like I was nothing, not worthy of your love, let alone the love of another person. You made me feel unworthy of love from a God that I was told didn't make mistakes and *that* gutted me most of all."

Her eyes glance around the parking lot, as if she is making sure no one can hear our conversation over the sound of the band. "I was wrong, honey. So wrong."

Keeping my own voice quiet, I lean in even closer to her. "You do *not* get to call me honey. You held my head underwater until I couldn't breathe—until my vision went black around the edges and I was forced to give in to the fleeting thought that I was about to die. All because *you* didn't believe that I was worthy of love because I was gay, and that by doing so, I would suddenly turn into the perfect, straight daughter who wouldn't embarrass you in front of your church friends. All because I loved a *woman*. How dare you track me down after all this time. Why are you even here? To try and convince me that I'm still going to hell? To rub it in my face that even after all these years that I'm not enough for you? That holding me under that water couldn't fail to accomplish the one thing you set out to do when you ripped me away from this community?"

My voice trembles, but I continue with all the unsaid words I've been holding onto for the past decade. "I was a teenager. I was already afraid of what it meant for my life that I was different from almost everyone else my age, and instead of helping me through it, you used it against me in the worst possible way. Because of that, you don't get to call me honey. You don't get to call me your daughter because I certainly don't think of you as my mother."

She gasps, and though I see the hurt in her eyes, I can't sit next to her another minute. I push to my feet, but she stops me before I can storm away.

"I came here to tell you that I left your father. And while I know that doesn't negate what happened to you and what I willingly put you through, I hope this can serve as the first small step toward rebuilding a relationship with you."

I pause for the briefest of seconds, not sure exactly what I'm waiting for her to say next. Am I expecting her to apologize? To fall to her feet and beg for teenage Esme's forgiveness even though I am now an adult? But in the end, she doesn't do any of those things.

Instead, she stands, giving me a sad smile as tears shine in her eyes. "I'm in town until next Thursday. If you can find it in your heart to talk to me, I'm at the Pelican Inn."

She reaches out a hand as if to touch me but thinks better of it at the last moment. Grasping her designer purse, she turns and walks in the opposite direction, leaving me in stunned silence and reeling with confusion.

Twenty-Five
Imogen

RUNNING ON FUMES THANKS TO THE SUCCESS OF THE DAY, I don't have a chance to sneak out of the shop until close to seven. You'd never know that the shops are winding down for the night with the way residents of Luna Harbor clammer about. Couples sway on what has become a makeshift dance floor in front of the stage, kids line up to get their faces painted, and fresh lemonade is still being squeezed at a nearby booth.

It's almost the perfect start to summer. If only Esme was at my side to enjoy these few minutes with me as the breeze blows across the lot instead of inside her own shop, where I'm sure she is up to her elbows with customers.

I soak in the atmosphere with a smile on my face, taking in the families and groups of friends that mill about. Noticing several of our regular customers, I make my way over to where they stand but am stopped before I make it to the ladies.

"Imogen!" I hear an almost panicked voice call out and whip around to find Aveline rushing up to me as quickly as her legs will carry her.

I meet her halfway, placing a hand on each of her biceps as if steadying her. "What's wrong?" I ask, unease settling low in my belly.

She's almost out of breath, and I coax her into taking a few deep inhalations before nodding at her to continue.

Even over the sound of the band, I can hear her voice as it cracks, sending chills down my spine. "It's Esme. She came back from getting something to eat about two hours ago looking like she had just seen a ghost. Said something happened and she needed to leave right away. I couldn't get it all out of her before she ran, but she said something about a woman named Patricia that had found her here. It's been so slammed at the dispensary that I haven't been able to find you, and when I finally had a chance to leave the shop, I went straight to yours. Birdie said you were out here somewhere, and I knew I had to find you."

My knees go weak, knocking together, and now it's Aveline that is holding me up. Voice small and shaky, I respond, "Pa... Patricia is her mother."

Aveline goes pale, her face draining of color much the way I'm sure mine already has. She holds onto me tighter and looks into my eyes. "I had no idea. I wouldn't have let her leave."

"Was she going somewhere to meet up with her?"

Shaking her head, she tells me that Esme simply said she had to leave for the rest of the evening, apologizing profusely for inconveniencing the store on the busiest day of the year.

Thanking her, I promise to find her before dashing back to The Grateful Thread and forgetting about my quest for fair-style food.

As quickly as I can, I pull Grandma Birdie to the back, explaining to her in haste what Aveline first conveyed to me. My grandmother pulls me into the tightest of hugs, patting the back of my head with her sun-dappled hand.

"Go and find our girl," she tells me before releasing me, dropping my car keys into my hand and pushing me toward the door. "Text me as soon as you hear anything."

I give her a small smile and head to my car, determined to find my girl, no matter what it takes.

On the way to her apartment, I pass the park and library, noticing that her car isn't parked at either spot. I make a quick pass through town, checking the parking lots of several of the restaurants we've visited over the last few months to no avail.

SEW INTO YOU   149

A short time later, I'm pulling my car into the driveway, and while I see her car, no lights are turned on in her small apartment over the garage. Still, I jog up the steps and bang on the door, hoping she is simply asleep.

I knock and bang, loudly calling her name.

But there is no response.

Hearing footsteps on the gravel drive, my hopes momentarily lift but deflate when I see Anita Farley at the bottom of the steps. "Imogen, darling, is that you?"

Climbing down from my perch at the top of the stairs, I confirm the landlady and retired librarian's question. "Hi, Mrs. Farley. I'm sorry for disturbing you."

"Oh, dear, not a bother at all. It isn't very often that we get visitors, even if they are unintentionally here to see us. You know, you get to be our age and find that more often than not, when someone comes to visit, it isn't for the best of reasons."

The woman, close in age to my grandmother, must sense that I'm not quite sure how to answer her last statement. Instead, she continues to speak. "I assume you're looking for that beautiful woman of yours who rents out the space up there?" She nods her head in the direction of the garage apartment, and I find myself nodding emphatically in return.

"Yes," I tell her. "I need to find her. Did you happen to see her when she got home?"

Mrs. Farley points with a gnarled, weathered finger to a small path that is carved in the trees behind her house. In all the times I've been here in the last few months, I've never noticed the path, but on closer inspection, it almost appears to be that way on purpose. "You follow that pathway, and I'm almost certain you'll find your beloved."

I clasp her hand in mine. "Thank you, Mrs. Farley."

"Please, dear," she tells me, "call me Anita. And be sure to stop over to say hi to me next time you're over. I'd love to share a sweet tea with you on the front porch."

I know thanks will never be enough, yet I thank the woman again before running off toward the pathway, desperate to find Esme wherever she ran off to.

Unsure of where the path leads, I pull up the flashlight on my phone and aim it at the ground. While it's not completely dark, the tree coverage provides shade, making it hard to see where I'm walking. Navigating through the trees, I watch in awe as they transform from thick pines and tall oaks into coastal palm trees and then into mangrove trees. Traipsing over the roots embedded in the sandy soil of nature's very own filtration system, I take off my ballet flats and continue along the walk, my now bare feet almost silent in the warm, shallow waters of the coast.

A small, sandy atoll juts out into the water and as I approach. Still being careful of the root systems underfoot, I can make out the silhouette of a woman sitting on the ground, her arms tightly clasped around her knees, smoke drifting off the joint firmly held between two fingers.

As I look around, I see several buildings in the distance that I know well, and I instantly realize that this is the little piece of land Esme and I used to point to as kids from across the bay. A place we always wanted to explore but could never find our way to. A place that was all but a mirage.

And now, my sad, beautiful girl is sitting alone in the sand in the very place we wanted so badly to explore as children.

I fire off a quick message to Aveline and Grandma Birdie, letting the women know I've located our runaway. Then, treating her like a skittish animal, I approach cautiously, sitting down next to her and mimicking her posture. Her big, beautiful eyes are red-rimmed, and even in the diminishing light of day, I can see the tear tracks that have streaked down her blotchy yet still beautiful face.

We sit in silence for several minutes, just existing in the same space as one another. And when I finally hold out my hand, she takes it without reluctance, our fingers immediately threading through one another to create that special bond that always brings us closer to one another.

When the sun has finally set, fully sinking beneath the horizon, I turn my body toward Esme, keeping our hands firmly clasped. "I heard you've had quite the eventful day."

She scoffs as if that's the understatement of the century, and to her credit, seeing her mother for the first time in years definitely counts as more than an eventful day.

The saltwater around us has slowly begun to rise in anticipation of high tide, our sandy little atoll growing smaller and smaller. I lay my head on Esme's shoulder, staring out at the water surrounding us. "Are we going to sit here until we wash away?"

"Somedays, I think that would be the easiest thing to do." I hear the hurt in her voice. The uncertainty and shame that is still buried somewhere deep inside.

I move even closer, pressing my right side firmly against her left, simply wanting her to feel the contact of my body. Wanting her to feel anchored to me, if even for a minute.

"Well," I tell her as she brings the now extinguished joint to her lips, relighting it with the flick of a Zippo lighter, "the way I see it, we have three choices."

Esme glances at me out of the corner of her eye, the first time she has looked at me since I sat down next to her on this secluded little island that will soon be gone as the water flows back into the bay.

She takes a long drag off the joint, and when I take it from her fingers, repeating the process myself, she finally fully turns to look at me, a question in her beautiful, somber eyes.

I cough a few times as I exhale, not used to the harsh smoke as it fills my lungs. And while I can't be certain, I think I see Esme's lips quirk up just the tiniest bit as she watches me. As I pass the tightly rolled paper back to her, I start laying out the options that I see fit.

"First, we could just sit here. Let the tide come up to our toes, let the water wash over us and carry us off into the sea where we no longer have to worry about things like parents, and jobs, and life. It sounds good, and if there was one person I would do that for, do that *with*, it would be you, my beautiful Esme. But I think we both have a lot of life left to live—lives to change and people to inspire. So, I don't think that letting ourselves succumb to a watery demise is quite the solution. I don't know about you, but I've personally never had any desire to see Davy Jones's Locker in the flesh."

She gives me a sound that's somewhere between a huff and a laugh. I take it as my sign to continue. "Second, we could forget the entire day happened. We can walk back to your apartment and get shit-faced wasted on cheap booze that we don't have to steal from my parents' refrigerator. I'm talking so damn drunk that we have to fight for room over the toilet bowl in the morning, the type of drunk that is usually saved for college kids when they move away from home the first time. But then again, we're not teenagers anymore and now that we're in our mid-twenties, it will probably take twice as long to recover and more than some greasy diner food. We'd surely miss out on work, and even more importantly, it wouldn't really solve anything."

Fully turning to look into my eyes, the tormented look I'm met with would be enough to knock me to my knees if I wasn't already seated. "And what's the third option?" Esme asks, her voice nothing more than a whisper.

"We walk back to your apartment, I make us each a nice, hot cup of tea with just a splash of whiskey, we curl up under our quilt, and as painful as it is to talk about, you tell me what happened. It can be just what happened today or what happened all those years ago. Esme, it's up to you to know when you're ready to share that story with me. But please believe me when I tell you that whatever happened in your past isn't what defines you as a person now."

There is nothing in this moment that I want more than to make her understand. To make her believe that she isn't broken or damaged, that her trauma is something she can overcome, and that I'll be there every step of the way, no matter the story she decides to tell.

"Let me be there for you, Esme," I tell her softly, leaning in enough to press my lips lightly against hers. "Let me be there for you as your friend, as your lover, as *your* person. Let me in, and if you fall apart in the process, trust that I'll be there to help put you back together."

Tears trail down my cheeks, and while I can't see them, I feel them as they fall against my chest, rolling down to be soaked up by the fabric of my dress. Sand coats my bare legs, and while I'm confident there is already some in my underwear, I'd be content to sit here all night if I could just get her to open up, sandy vagina be damned.

The water is now almost at our toes, our little island shrinking more and more. Pushing against the sand, I stand fully, brushing off my legs before reaching a hand out to Esme. "You don't have to do this alone. It's not you against the world now, love. It's us against the world, and what a powerful force we are."

Her eyes bounce between my face and my hand several times, the moonlight illuminating the flecks of gold that are scattered throughout the rich, dark brown of her irises. And just as I'm beginning to lose faith that she'll reach out, taking the help I am offering, she slips her hand into mine and pushes herself up, out of the sand.

Tears in her own eyes, she wraps her arms around me in a bone-crushing hug. Esme holds on to me as if I'm a mirage, willing to disappear at any moment and without notice. One hand comes to tangle in my hair, and a small sob escapes her as she inhales into the crook of my neck.

Finally, while still wrapped in her tight embrace, she whispers into my ear…

"Option three."

Twenty-Six
Esme

ARRIVING AT MY APARTMENT, IMOGEN USHERS ME UP THE STAIRS
with a confident yet soft hand to my lower back. I push open the
door and walk into the kitchen, waiting for her to join me at the
counter.

Still standing in the doorway, she calls out, "You don't lock
your door?"

I give her a small shrug. "It's Luna Harbor. When was the
last time something bad happened here?"

Always a relatively safe place, Luna Harbor has been named
one of the safest cities in the United States for the past four years
running. Before that, it was a notable mention for at least a
decade. Its safety record was one of the initial reasons my
parents chose to move here back when I was a child. At the end
of the day, who could have imagined that those two very people
who moved to a town based on its crime statistics would be the
most unsafe people for me to be around? Now, with promises of
salvation and a reconciliation with my mother forefront in my
mind, I pull two cups from the cabinet and go about setting the
kettle over the stove.

Imogen enters the small yet functional kitchen, taking over
the work of finding tea bags and setting one in each mug. "Go
get comfortable and grab me something of yours to change into.
I'm not staying in this dress all night."

I follow her simple command, grabbing a ratty old tank top
and pair of sweatpants for myself before finding another outfit

for Imogen to change into. There is still some sand on my legs, and I stand in my tiny shower to wipe it away—hoping to not get much between the sheets of my bed.

It's a hazard of coastal living that I'm glad to deal with. Because each grain of sand helps to remind me of where I am, of who I am with, and of the woman I know I can be for her.

I watch Imogen as she enters my room a short while later, a mug in each hand. She sets both mugs on my nightstand, the steam wafting into the air around us to lightly scent my room with the comforting aroma of bergamot and Earl Grey tea.

Not bothering to move to the bathroom, she pulls her dress up and over her head before folding it neatly, placing it on the edge of my bed. Imogen peels her bra and underwear off her body, and while I'm still waging an emotional battle in my mind, I can't help but take a moment to enjoy her curves.

My shirt is tighter on her than it is over my own slim frame, pulling taut across her breasts. Her nipples pebble under the worn fabric, and I have to stop myself from reaching out to brush the pad of my thumb across the little peaks. Without words, she slides into my sweats, pulling the elastic waistband up and over her beautiful, thick hips. Then, Imogen walks around my bed, gently tugging back the quilt and sheets before gesturing for me to climb in.

The light is dim in the room, a simple table lamp illuminating the space in a soft, amber hue. I obey her command, silently slipping between the sheets before Imogen joins me. Passing a mug of tea to her before I take my own, we sip in relative silence, the only sound coming from the crickets and frogs singing their nightly songs.

She doesn't rush me. Doesn't push for me to speak or urge me to spill my long-hidden secrets. Instead, she stares into her mug of tea as if all the world's answers are held within the cup while waiting for me to gather the courage to begin.

And after several long, silent minutes, I do just that.

"Do you remember the night of our tenth-grade formal dance?"

She gives me a nod along with a little sound of confirmation.

"You had on that long, bubblegum pink dress with a slit up to your thigh. Your hair was perfectly styled in a half-up half-down type of thing with loose curls, and all I wanted to do was run my fingers through them all night long."

She places her mug on the floor next to the bed before taking my hand in hers, and I allow the contact of her warm skin to ground me in this moment instead of hurtling me back to the past as I continue to speak.

"We were always careful, *so* careful. And honestly, I don't think either of us really cared what others thought of us, as individuals or as a pair. Maybe we weren't ready to tell our parents, but I know, at least for me, I wouldn't have cared if our friends knew how in love with you I was." I give her a small smile, though I'm sure it doesn't quite reach my eyes. "That night, we snuck off into a side hallway together, wanting desperately to share at least one slow dance in each other's arms. I'll never forget swaying in time to the music, you softly singing along to the lyrics of a song I've long since forgotten."

I feel her hand in mine, and I study the weight, still using it to tether me to the present. "But I wasn't careful enough that night because someone saw us. To this day, I'm not sure who it was, but someone saw us in the hallway, and as our lips pressed against each other, they took a picture." Imogen gasps in surprise, and I wish this was where the story ended.

But this is only the beginning.

"That picture got into the hands of my father the same night. He was always stern; I'm sure you remember as much. It's why I always preferred to spend weekends at your house over mine—I felt like I could actually have *fun* when I was at your house. That I could be a kid. But still, as stern as he was, I always thought it was simply that he wanted the best for me as his only child. At least that is what he led me to believe. But that weekend, when I came home from staying over at your house after the dance, everything had changed.

"It was the first time he ever raised a hand to me, the first time he ever hit me. He held his phone screen centimeters from my face, forcing me to stare at our picture while going on and on about how not only was his daughter a whore, but a whore who wasn't even good enough to whore around with a man. Then, when he ran out of words to say, he slapped me across the face, phone still in hand. I had never heard him use such words before that day, and never in any nightmare I could have concocted did I expect they would be aimed at me."

I laugh, but there is no humor behind the sound. "I swear, I had the outline of that phone on my cheek for a solid three days. Monday morning came and I got ready for school like I always did. I came down the stairs and into the kitchen to find both of my parents seated at the table. My mom had tears in her eyes, and they were so bloodshot that I couldn't tell where her irises stopped and the whites of her eyes began. It was like she hadn't slept for weeks and instead spent every hour of the day crying.

"My father forced me to the table and told me that I would not be going back to that horrible school that filled my head with wild ideas of what normalcy was. That he and my mother *prayed* about it, prayed about *me*, and that the solution they agreed upon was to move back to Nebraska."

Braving a glance as Imogen, our hands still clasped together, I watch a tear roll down her cheek as the puzzle pieces of my disappearance begin to snap into place.

"I screamed and cried—so hard that I vomited all over the kitchen table and floor before I was forced to clean it up as they watched. If there were any words that I could have said that would have changed his mind, I would have said them. But it was no use. I could have yelled until I was blue in the face, and he wouldn't have changed his mind. We left that day without packing as much as an overnight bag. A few days later, all our things from the house in Luna Harbor arrived. I unpacked my boxes at my mother's request as if I were on autopilot, like a zombie going through the motions as fear of the unknown held me down. The very last box I opened, carefully using scissors to slice across the packing tape while watching for my fingers, felt like it was a sign. That I was going to have to fight like hell to get away, but that somehow, I would find my way back to where I was supposed to be. And when I opened that box and saw our quilt folded neatly on top, I knew that where I was supposed to be was with you.

"I wasn't allowed to have my phone, no access to a computer unless I was supervised. I knew your address, but was too terrified to even try to write. I was to go to school and church with barely nothing else in between. I came home from school each day and did my schoolwork, trying my damndest not to make waves. And each night, I would climb into my bed and hold that quilt tightly to my chest, quietly sobbing as your scent dissipated over time."

My own tears fall now, and I let them, needing the heavy catharsis they provide. I take another sip of my tea, now tepid and bitter from the tannins in the tea bag, and I chuckle to myself when I notice how the flavor of the tea now matches my own severely bitter mood.

Imogen opens her mouth, like she is getting ready to speak, but I stop her with a gentle touch. "Please let me finish."

She nods.

"We had only been back in Nebraska for a few months, but I already knew that I had to leave as soon as I possibly could. It wasn't just about getting back to you—although that was always my end goal. It was about the increasing rage that continued to build inside my father, the way he constantly looked at me with nothing but disgust. I was forced into therapy for my *condition*, as my mother called it, only to find out that the man I had been speaking to wasn't actually a licensed medical professional, but was, in fact, a member of my parents' church."

I slide further down in my bed, my head resting on Imogen's chest. Immediately, her fingers delve into my hair, and she continues to sift her digits through the strands in languid, comforting strokes.

She doesn't stop as I tell her about the reparative therapies my parents forced upon me, and while I'm deeply thankful that their measures never stooped to full-on conversion therapy in the most well-known sense of the term, I know now as an adult that their methods were not any less harmful.

Imogen's body trembles beneath mine as I tell her about the involuntary baptisms I was forced to endure—how breathing got harder the more I struggled, how the saltwater of my tears mixed with the water of the vessel I was forced into, how I found myself sucking in lungfuls of water as the sobs wracked my body, and how many times, I prayed to God to simply let me die.

Her hand continues to weave through my hair when I tell her about my breaking point. When I tell her about stealing from my own family, pawning whatever I could before leaving without so much as a glance backward—only a few personal items and my treasured quilt in my hands.

While she never interrupts me, I can tell she's crying from the way her body shakes against mine. It's in the way quiet little sobs escape when I tell her about the nights I spent sleeping at chilly bus stops or in public parks and in the way small sniffles echo through the room as I tell her about the day I literally ran tray-first into Aveline after running out of money somewhere in the middle of Colorado, desperate to find my way back to Luna Harbor.

I move into lighter subjects—the friendship I formed with Aveline, the first studio apartment I shared with her, my first job with High Tide. We talk about the difference cannabis has made in my life—both personally and professionally. It's a welcomed reprieve from the gravity of the serious monologue of the last hour, and as I continue to tell her about my time between finding myself in Colorado and returning to Luna Harbor, I find that I'm smiling.

"So," Imogen finally says after a long silence, "Patricia is here?"

She ends the sentence as a half-question half-statement, already knowing the answer to her question.

My head nods of its own volition, my curls frizzing out around me from the near constant fingers that have been combing through them. "I was honestly just so shocked to see her that I don't think I could have formed a coherent sentence if my life depended on it. I know I spoke heatedly to her, but thank God no one else could hear us over the sounds of the band. She told me she was here because she left my dad. Like I'm supposed to suddenly just be okay with whatever role it was she played in my pain because she left my father, like I was supposed to jump into her arms and cry tears of joy at having a mother after almost ten years of being utterly alone."

Imogen slides down the mattress and pulls me into her arms. She gives me a kiss, nothing more than a simple meeting of lips, but it is enough to show me that she is still here for me. *With* me. That she doesn't feel any less for me now she did at the beginning of this conversation. That I'm not broken or damaged beyond repair like I still sometimes feel I am. That for once in my life, I truly am not alone the way I feared I would be for the rest of my life.

Facing one another, she keeps her arms locked around me, gently trailing her fingers up and down the length of my back in no particular pattern. "Thank you for sharing all of that with me tonight. I know it couldn't have been an easy thing to do."

There isn't an ounce of pity in her emerald-green gaze, but instead, a kind compassion resides there, the likes of which I've never seen from someone outside of my Imogen. She holds me tighter, only moving her arm to shift the quilt higher up our bodies.

"Besides," she says after several silent minutes, "when it comes to your mom, you don't have to make any decisions tonight. You don't owe her anything, sweetie. If you decide you don't want to hear her out while she is here, I certainly wouldn't blame you. Then again, if you do decide you want to hear her out, I wouldn't blame you for that either. The decision is yours alone to make, but I'll be here to talk through it with you or support you in any way I can."

My eyes begin to water again, this time in unfiltered gratitude for the guardian angel in front of me. And as the night wanes on and we continue to hold onto each other tightly, we drift off to sleep together with no nightmares in sight.

Twenty-Seven

Luna Sea Plaza
Owner's Chat

MAEVE: Thank you all for making the third annual Luna Sea Lunacy such a success! We had more people than ever this year!

SUNDAY: It was fantastic! We sold out of a ton of things. Going to need to do a big reorder this week!

CAMPBELL: Agreed. It was a wonderful day.

WATSON: Holy hell, did Campbell just give you a roundabout compliment about your event?

WATSON: Hashtag Winning.

OAKEN: Not how hashtags work, old man.

CAMPBELL: A wonderful day for my store is all I meant.

HOLLIS: No backtracking now, Cam.

SUNDAY: Dare I say that I even saw you smile today?

CAMPBELL: I smile all the time.

SUNDAY: If by smile, you mean grimace.

OAKEN: She's not lying, man.

WATSON: You often look like you have gas.

MAEVE: *Laughing emoji*

WATSON: Bad gas.

CAMPBELL: And this is why I stay away from all of you.

SUNDAY: Truly though, my daughter loved the time she spent in your store and is a bit miffed that I never brought her in before now.

CAMPBELL: Well, Miss Rosie can come back to visit any time she would like.

HOLLIS: Awww, Cammy Boy has a soft side!

CAMPBELL: Only because she is too young to constantly inundate me with unnecessary text messages.

WATSON: Hashtag spoilsport.

Twenty-Eight
Imogen

DAWN IS JUST BREAKING WHEN I WAKE, MY ARMS AND LEGS tangled around Esme as she snores quietly next to me. The room around us is dark, the first light of day not making it into the apartment quite yet. Still, I can make out the gentle slope of Esme's nose and the way her eyelashes fan out across her cheeks as her soft exhales tickle my face, mere inches from hers.

I think back on last night, on the stories she *finally* shared with me, and my heart breaks all over again for my beautiful, sweet girl. I can't begin to fathom how horrible her experiences were, how afraid she must have felt, and how alone her family forced her into believing she had to be.

And here and now, under the quilt we shared as children, I vow that she will never feel that way again.

Because my Esme deserves all the love in the world.

My phone chirps from my handbag, and I gently extract myself from Esme and the bed. Padding out to the living room to find my purse, I dig around until I come up victorious, silencing the notification chime before sliding across the screen to read the text messages that have come through.

BIRDIE: Don't you even think of coming into work today.

BIRDIE: Aveline says the same thing for Esme.

BIRDIE: You just stay and take care of our girl.

BIRDIE: Spoke with Anita. She is going to leave you fixings for breakfast.

BIRDIE: Help that beautiful girl mend her heart, and I'll see you tomorrow.

BIRDIE: Love you, sweetheart.

I can't help but smile, soaking in the love of my own family. Only this morning, it feels slightly bittersweet. However, I'm thankful that now, Esme gets to feel their love, too.

Responding to Birdie, I then shoot off a text to Aveline to make sure she is on board with me keeping Esme all to myself today. Next, I send a quick early morning message to Maeve, a secret plan forming in my mind.

Quietly, I open the front door, smiling at the three large bags of groceries that are perched atop the stoop. Bringing them inside, I scan through cabinets and drawers looking for pans and whisks, plates and forks, before laying out all the ingredients on the kitchen counter.

Mrs. Farley certainly didn't skimp, including everything from coffee grounds and orange juice to thick slabs of fresh-cut bacon and eggs that I'm confident came from one of her neighbors, who keeps chickens in their backyard.

I turn on some soft music and hum along, cracking eggs into a silver bowl and whisking ingredients together for pancakes. Splitting the batter in half, I add in a handful of blueberries into one half while adding chocolate chips to the other.

The tantalizing scent of bacon and freshly-brewed coffee fills the small apartment while sunlight begins to pour in through the windows.

Happily singing along to Taylor Swift—the person, not the cat—I can feel the instant Esme enters the room. The air turning thick around us, I turn to face her. I find her smiling at me through sleep-mussed hair and half-awake eyes, watching intently as I sway and sing along to the song *Lover*.

Giving a little shimmy, I walk to where she stands and pull her into my arms. With my fingers caressing her back, we sway together, listening to the words as they wash over us, echoing all the words I want to say to her. I run my nose along her neck before lightly pressing kisses up the same path.

"Good morning, my love," I tell her softly.

She answers with a voice equally as sleep-mussed as her bedhead. "Any morning that I wake up with you in my apartment is a good morning."

The sizzle of the stovetop grabs my attention, and with a quick kiss to her lips, I push away, rushing to remove the bacon before it turns from ideally crispy to a pile of charred crumbs.

Pointing to the stools that sit neatly tucked under the small, kitchen island, I instruct her to sit, filling up a mug with hot coffee and placing it in front of her. "We're not going to work today."

Esme looks skeptical as I add a glass of orange juice to her place setting. "What do you mean? I'm due in at ten."

"Not today, you're not!" I flip the last pancake and stack it neatly with the rest of them on Esme's plate. Then, I add a few slices of bacon and some delightfully fluffy scrambled eggs. Making a second plate for myself, only with chocolate chip pancakes instead of blueberry, I take a seat next to her and dig in. "I've talked to both Birdie and Aveline, and they agreed that it would be best if we took a mental health day. Wasn't my idea, but I can't say I'm upset about it."

"Really?" She sounds hopeful when she asks, and it squeezes at my heart. Most of the time, Esme is a strong woman who is hell-bent on traversing life on her own, but in times like these, when she speaks her word so softly, it's almost as if she is still a child, seeking love and acceptance wherever she can find it.

Somehow, I'll make her see that my love and acceptance doesn't come with conditions.

That she is already perfect exactly how she is.

"Yeah," I tell her with a smile. "So, what do you want to do today? Want to take me back to the atoll so I can see it in the daylight?"

A misty, faraway look creeps over her face, like she's remembering something from long ago before a flash of understanding settles over her. "Holy shit! That's the place we used to see from across the bay, isn't it?"

Nostalgia overtakes me, and I'm a small girl again, giggling alongside Esme as we point to the small atoll and talk about it being the perfect place to run away to. The perfect place to call our little slice of home. We were determined that all we needed was a fort and some fishing poles and that we could make it into our own little, secret paradise.

Of course, this was before either of us ever learned about how the ocean actually works. About things like low and high tides and how the gravitational pull of the moon causes the depth at any given point in time to fluctuate.

Thinking back on those past science lessons now, they hold many parallels to real life, and I smile fondly at that knowledge. Luna Harbor—moon harbor—while Esme and I are the tides, ebbing and flowing until we finally find each other, crashing back into one another like the frenetic sea during a tropical storm.

"It is," I finally tell her. "I knew it the second I saw it. How much time did we spend obsessing over that little spot of sand? Never realizing that it would sink and rise into the sea with each passing day."

She laughs, probably also picturing us as two small girls, yearning to run and play in the white sand. "Let's do it. We can run to the store and pack a picnic, then swing by your apartment and grab one of your suits on the way back."

With excitement, I push to my feet, ready to forget about the rest of my breakfast in favor of a day of adventure with the girl I love.

Together, we make quick work of the dishes, rinsing and loading them into the dishwasher while laughing and smiling the entire time.

As we enter Esme's bedroom a short time later, she comes up behind me, wrapping her arms around my torso and pressing her front to my back. "I love the way you look in my clothes," she croons against my ear.

Her voice sends shivers down my spine, as it often does, and I know if I ruminate on the feeling for too long, we'll never leave this bedroom again.

We quietly dress—Esme in her bathing suit and coverup, me in my clothes from last night—and as we're getting ready to leave the apartment, she stops, darting back into the kitchen to scrawl something on a piece of paper. Tucking it into the pocket of her coverup, she joins me and we walk down the stairs before climbing into my car.

"Can we stop at the Pelican Inn on our way back?"

"Isn't that where…" I trail off, not wanting to break the easy way our morning has flowed.

Esme nods, placing her hand on my thigh as I continue to drive, almost as if she is seeking comfort in the connection between our bodies. "I decided I'm not ready to hear her out yet. The feelings that she brought back by showing up here unannounced, they are everything I fight to run from almost daily. Still, I can't let her just sit at the inn and wonder if I'm ever going to show."

My right hand drops from the wheel while my left stays planted, steering us along our journey. I link my fingers with hers, giving a little squeeze, letting her know that I am here for her. "You're the bravest person I know, Esme, and you have to do what is best for your mental health. I'll stand behind you with whatever decision you make. But I will say, I think it is wise of you to take this on your timetable and not hers."

I love the smile she gives me in return. There is still a slight hint of sadness around the edges, but the reverence that overtakes it leaves me awestruck. Never did I think I would see this woman again—my love, my entire heart. Yet, here she is, staring at me as if I'm some mythical deity as we navigate this new chapter together.

"In my note, I asked if she would leave her phone number with the front desk for me before she leaves. It's what I can give her right now, the hope that maybe one day I'll be able to speak with her. To open up freely and move forward with some semblance of a relationship. But right now, it's the best I can do."

"Sometimes," I tell her in response, "the best you can do is more than enough."

She squeezes my fingers again, and I return the gesture, letting her know I'm still here for her. Still here *with* her.

Twenty-Nine

Luna Sea Plaza
Owner's Chat

MAEVE: What would you guys think of hosting more events throughout the year like Luna Sea Lunacy?

MAEVE: A bit smaller in scale, of course.

ESME: Like more sales and events that correspond throughout the stores in the plaza?

MAEVE: EXACTLY!

OAKEN: The correct time to type in all caps.

WATSON: I've told you a million times, I wasn't doing it on purpose.

HOLLIS: Do you have any thoughts about specific days or times of the year to celebrate?

SUNDAY: Christmas in July?

CAMPBELL: I don't celebrate Christmas.

MAEVE: Might be a little soon to have an event in July.

MAEVE: Back to school in August/September?

IMOGEN: *GIF of woman yawning*

SUNDAY: Too boring. We need to do something fun.

SUNDAY: Salsa day? Featuring different local salsa recipes and salsa dancing?

ESME: How about a progressive party where each store features a signature drink and appetizer to share with customers?

OAKEN: We could each theme our treats to fit our business.

WATSON: I do enjoy a nice, cold beverage from time to time.

CAMPBELL: And how would you suggest booze and snacks fit into a toy store?

CAMPBELL: Teddy Bear Day is in September and would pair nicely with back-to-school sales.

OAKEN: Teddy Bear Day?

HOLLIS: Hummm...I have a few things that could cater to a different type of bear...

IMOGEN: *GIF of man saying rawr*

Thirty
Esme

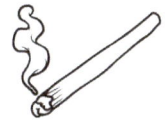

SOMEHOW, IN THE LAST TEN YEARS, I HAVE MANAGED TO FORGET just how brutal the summer heat of Florida can be. It's relentless in its humidity, and no matter how I try to tame my hair on hot, summer days, I wind up looking like Monica from *Friends* at the end of each day, just like in that one episode where the gang travels to Barbados.

Thank God for cute hats because they're the only thing saving me from looking like a rat crawled on top of my head to build its nest on most days.

Imogen comes out of my bathroom, a wide-tooth comb in hand and a towel wrapped loosely around her torso before taking a seat behind me on my bed. She widens her legs, pulling me between them before softly bringing the comb to my wet-from-the-shower-hair.

Starting at the very ends, she works through my tangles with great care, continually checking that she isn't being too harsh on my scalp. We talk about everything and nothing as she works, chatting about work and her family, about who we think is hooking up with each other at the plaza, and things we both want to check off our bucket list before the summer ends. For me, it's paddle-boarding in the bay, while Imogen dreams of sleeping on the beach, just her and I under a starry night's sky.

It feels magical to be here between her legs, having her care for me in such a simple way. I realize that it has been years since I've had someone show me love in such a beautiful way, that each one of her touches and caresses is filled with a tenderness I had desperately been missing.

While she continues to work on my hair, I rub my hands up and down her smooth legs. They're touched by the sun after a rare day off spent together on the sands of our private atoll, and even with a cool shower, her skin is warm to the touch. I know we're meeting our friends in just over an hour, yet I can't stop myself from continuing to silently tease her skin as she works through the various knots in my hair.

Imogen pushes up from the bed upon completion, but before she can walk away, I grab her wrist, holding her in place. She turns to look at me, her green eyes knocking into my chest with the force of a two-ton wrecking ball.

"Thank you," I tell her softly, her wrist still in my hand.

"For what?" she replies.

Pulling her back to where I am seated, I position myself at the edge of the mattress, giving her the space to step between my outstretched thighs. "For taking care of me. For loving me."

Biting her bottom lip, she smiles at me while looping her arms around my neck. "It's all I've ever wanted to do in life. I know so many women who have this urge to have kids. To nurture little babies into successful, thriving adults. But even when we were young, I never had any desire other than to take care of you. To be there for you and build you up, to make you realize what a beautiful, wonderful person you are. I still want that now. It's all I want, Esme. To love you."

Her eyes are misty, as I'm sure mine are, too. This woman—this perfect woman—still wants me, still wants to *love* me. Even after so many people made me feel like I wasn't worthy of love. It's a precious gift I'll never take for granted. And the thought is enough to send shivers over my body. While they could be caused by the combination of sun and the apartment's air conditioning, I know that neither of those external factors caused this feeling, that this is all Imogen's doing.

And perhaps, even more importantly, the bombshell standing in front of me, all pink from the sun, wants my love just as desperately as I want hers.

Imogen steps back, and this time, instead of reaching for her wrist, I reach for the white, cotton towel tucked around her body. Plucking at the small knot, it tumbles to the ground, settling in a puddle on the faded, blue, bedroom carpet. She gasps but makes no move to cover her body from my sight.

"Come here, beautiful," I tell her through the heavy emotion building in my throat.

Without hesitation, she comes back to her place between my thighs, and my hands wrap around her hips as if they were made to rest there.

Maybe they were.

She's so fucking beautiful, bared to me like this. But then again, I don't think she could ever not be beautiful. Freshly showered like she is now or first thing in the morning with mussed hair and morning breath, I love the way she looks in both instances as well as every other second of the day.

I drop my hands, laying back on the mattress, legs still dangling over the edge. "Come ride my face, sweetheart. I want to meet our friends for dinner with your taste still on my lips. I want to memorize your flavor so I can dream about it more vividly than I already do each night."

A light blush creeps across her already sun-kissed cheeks, and I love that I can still make her flush with words alone. She scurries up my body, a leg on either side of my torso, and when she is inches from my mouth, Imogen leans back, pushing her cunt nearer to my waiting lips.

Already, I can smell her arousal. The distinct mixture of feminine musk and fresh cream wafts together to create a tantalizing scent unique to Imogen alone.

Again, my hands find her hips as I scoot down, finally connecting with her hot center. My tongue comes out to lick over her folds, a low moan echoing around us as I suck her clit into my mouth. I eat her pussy like I'm starved, and with each of Imogen's moans, I quicken my pace.

"This is all I ever wanted," she pants from above me, her back arched so prettily, those perfect tits on full display. "You, Esme. It's only ever been you. It's why I didn't go through with my engagement, why I *couldn't* go through with it." Her hips buck against me, rubbing her pussy over my face with frantic need. "Deep down inside, I knew you'd come back to me. I knew you'd find me, and I knew that once you did, I would never be able to let you go again."

Even if my mouth was free, I'd be at a loss for words

I double down on my efforts, licking and laving as her sweet juices flood my taste buds. And though I'm in my favorite place where I know my voice will be muffled, absolutely buried in Imogen's pussy, I growl against her regardless. "Give it all to me, sweetheart. Let me taste how much you love me. Let me taste what I do to you because *mother fucker*, I'm never letting you go again either."

Imogen screams into the room, a guttural noise from deep within the depths of her soul as she ruts her hips back and forth over my face. Tighter and tighter, I grasp her hips, nearly certain she'll be left with replicas of my fingerprints on her skin. She soaks me with her scent, leaving traces on my lips and chin, my nose and cheeks. And I don't even care. Hell, she could drown me with her flavors, and I'd be a willing participant. Unlike the watery torture of my past, this, I would willingly repeat every day for the rest of my life.

Her body tenses on top of me as I spear her with my tongue, sliding it in and out of her in deep, rhythmic strokes, and when she screams again, this time, it's my name.

"Esme!" she chants. Over and over again, she says my name mixed with a chorus of "I love you," and "I'll never leave you." And it's the most selfless thing she could do, giving me the reassurance and love that I need instead of giving into her own pleasure in a greedy way.

Imogen finally collapses on top of me, her belly meeting my face for a brief second, before rolling over into a boneless heap of glorious nakedness on my bed. She pants, still searching for breath while I lick my lips, already missing the warmth of her cunt on my face.

Her lips are warm when she presses them against mine, and I groan into her kiss, knowing if I let her go any further, we'll never make it to our friends. And while there is nothing I'd rather have than endless hours with Imogen in my bed, I don't want to let the others down either.

"Come on, sweetheart," I tell her, pushing up from the bed. "We don't want to keep our friends waiting, do we?"

The mock pout she throws my way is adorable, and it makes me laugh as she climbs out of bed lazily behind me. "You can't just eat me like a dang Little Debbie Snack Cake and expect me to recover so quickly! I feel like I just got off a cruise ship."

Her words are confirmed as she teeters around my bedroom, looking like Bambi on new legs. Imogen walks to my small closet and pulls a dress from a hanger before slipping it over her head. I'm not sure when she began keeping a few changes of clothes at my apartment, but I don't mind it. In fact, I love every second of seeing our clothes hanging together on the metal rod, cohabitating and mingling together in a space where her bright colors hang next to my mostly-neutral wardrobe.

It's a true study in both of our personalities. While Imogen is the life of the party, making friends quickly wherever we go, I prefer to hang on the sidelines, not drawing attention to myself. Being with Immy has given me the opportunity to push my own self-imposed boundaries, helping me to come out of the shell I pushed myself into for years as I struggled to come to terms with who I was.

A bright, paisley pattern in cool, jewel tones covers the dress

Imogen chose for today, and as it glides over her body, I immediately miss the sight of her curves now hidden by the flowing fabric.

I take my turn getting dressed, opting for loose-fitting jeans and a graphic tee—this one with a cartoon alpaca that reads *Alpaca 'Nother Bowl*. Looking in the mirror, I laugh, noticing that Imogen's hard work at detangling my tresses was all for naught. The rat's nest is back in full force, but it was all worth it to have her weight on top of me, her taste on my tongue as we chased her pleasure together.

In fact, everything up to this point was worth it. The pain and suffering I endured, the hateful words and hurtful actions—it was all worth it because it brought me back to the place I was truly always meant to be.

Everything with Imogen is worth it.

Thirty-One

Luna Sea Plaza
Owner's Chat

HOLLIS: What do you call a fly on a marijuana plant?

MAEVE: …

OAKEN: I've got nothing.

HOLLIS: A High Flyer!

ESME: *Clapping emoji* Oh, that's good. I approve.

IMOGEN: *GIF of Snoop Dog laughing*

HOLLIS: Seriously though, last night was a blast.

SUNDAY: Agreed! I don't know the last time I laughed so hard.

SUNDAY: I actually peed my pants a little at one point.

SUNDAY: Don't ever have kids.

HOLLIS: Kegels, Sunday. It's all about the Kegels.

HOLLIS: I also have a few toys you can insert to strengthen your pelvic floor.

HOLLIS: Some of them even have games built in!

CAMPBELL: Rosie is adorable. Surely that is worth the slight, occasional bladder weakness.

CAMPBELL: However, I hope she wasn't present if your night was full of the debauchery it sounds like was part of the evening.

MAEVE: HE SPEAKS!

SUNDAY: OMG you guys. Forget I mentioned it.

SUNDAY: And don't you worry, Cam. My little peanut was with her grandma, far away from any debauchery, so I don't think you have to call protective services on me.

HOLLIS: Ohhh, does the Cantankerous Campbell have a soft spot for children?

CAMPBELL: They don't ask such asinine questions all day long.

SUNDAY: HA! Spend a full day with my daughter and you'll be singing a different tune.

CAMPBELL: Unlikely. Bring her over anytime.

SUNDAY: Are you offering to babysit?

CAMPBELL: That isn't what I said.

ESME: Hey, not to ruin this beautiful moment, but has anyone heard from Watson this morning?

OAKEN: He and Birdie looked to be getting quite comfortable with one another in the parking lot when I was leaving.

IMOGEN: Oh. My. God.

IMOGEN: Gross.

IMOGEN: *GIF of woman screaming my eyes*

OAKEN: You weren't the one who had to see it.

OAKEN: In. The. Flesh.

MAEVE: Oh, come on, the two of them together would be super cute!

IMOGEN: That's my GRANDMOTHER!

HOLLIS: Pleasure doesn't have to stop when you reach a certain age.

HOLLIS: Sex is for everyone of age who wants it.

HOLLIS: Even you, Campbell.

CAMPBELL: I do just fine, but thank you for your concern.

Thirty-Two
Imogen

THANKS TO MY AMAZING NETWORK OF FRIENDS, MOST OF WHOM work at the plaza, I've been able to sneak around Esme for the last few weeks while carefully crafting details of a plan I hope shows her how much she means to me.

The surprise to end all surprises.

And no, I'm not asking her to marry me.

Yet.

Although, I would absolutely marry her today if given the opportunity. Hell, I would have married her at fifteen if I could have.

Maeve sits across from me in the bookstore, a spiral-bound notebook with dinosaurs on the cover, flipped open to reveal a to-do list a mile long.

"I talked to Principal Stein and confirmed we can use the gym. She really drove a hard bargain, and in exchange, you'll be working the snack stand at most home football games this fall, but all things considered, it could have gone much worse."

I laugh, thinking of the times spent in Luna Harbor High—more specifically the times spent in Principal Stein's office. While I wasn't often in trouble, I tended to live the *go big or go home* motto to its fullest after Esme left. I didn't have my best friend with me anymore, didn't have my girl by my side for all the ugliness that can be thrown at a sixteen-to-eighteen-year-old queer girl in a small, coastal town. So, I acted out in stupid ways —creating a giant slip and slide down the hallway of the athletic department, sticking over fifteen thousand plastic forks into the football field the night before our biggest game of the season, filling Principal Stein's office with enough balloons to send the house from *Up* floating into the sky.

In hindsight, everything I ever experienced pales in comparison to what Esme faced on a daily basis, and it still pains me to know that a picture of the two of us was the catalyst for her parents' hate. Deep down, I know none of it was my fault that they found out, but I still can't help but feel partially responsible for how she was treated.

"No drugs or alcohol allowed on the premises, but we both already knew that. Guess we'll just have to hold one hell of an after-party."

Already giddy at the thought of an adults-only after-party, I rub my hands together as if I'm some sort of evil mastermind scheming. "Let's do it on the beach! A big bonfire, drinks and snacks, music playing under the stars. Oh, I love this so much!"

We laugh and talk, going over more of the plans for what will be Luna Harbor's first ever LGBTQIA+ Prom. After talking with Esme and hearing what started her hellacious time spent under her parents' roof, knowing she never got to fully experience so many of the things I did, I decided I wanted to give back. Not only to her but to other kids in our town who might be facing issues at home or school, too. I only hope that reliving our only dance together helps to replace the memories she has and doesn't send her to a negative place.

There is no denying the fact that I had a relatively easy coming out story, not that it is something someone does only once. Truly, it is something that happens as a queer person almost daily. I've lost count of the number of times a salesperson or server has asked me if I'm waiting for my *husband*, how many times I've had to explain to a doctor that there really is no chance that I am pregnant and didn't need a urine test to prove it because, at the time, I was in a monogamous relationship with another woman.

Over and over, again and again. It's frustrating and embarrassing at times, while veering into slightly inhumane at others. The scoffs received when telling someone for the third time on the same day that no, the woman I'm with isn't my sister, she's my partner. The curious glances that are thrown my way as I walk down the street, simply holding the hand of the woman I love.

Truly, I'm beyond fortunate to call Luna Harbor home because I know there are many places across the country and around the world that are nowhere near as accepting as my community has become. Still, if I can help to bring some teens a much-needed safe space that I would have loved to have at their age, even if just for one night, I'm sure as hell going to do it. Especially if it is something I can share with Esme at the same time.

Maeve and I work through the list in tandem—sending emails to local businesses and vendors, reaching out to friends and family who work with at-risk youth, and concocting a plan for me to surprise Esme on the night of the event. Going back through way too many years of Facebook photo albums, I've been able to find some pictures from the dance I'm hoping to recreate and have matched the exact ugly shade of purple and silver used throughout—a nod to the Luna Harbor Wildcats.

Maeve's mid-sentence when a bell tinkles over the door, announcing the arrival of a customer. Turning to see what has her normal smile quickly morphing into a megawatt grin, I'm surprised to find not one, but two men I recognize approaching the counter we've claimed as our workspace.

"There's the two most handsome men in the world!" she exclaims, walking from around the counter to place a kiss on her husband, Sebastian's, lips. "How was lunch, you two?"

Sebastian smiles back at his wife, stars in his eyes. "Delicious," he says with a voice that's all smoke and gravel. And while he says the word in answer to Maeve's question, he's staring directly at the second man when he says it.

Aiden approaches carefully, giving a small wave to both of us. A blush creeps up his cheeks when he looks at me, and I'd pay any amount of money to know what's going on in that pretty, little head of his right this second.

While young, there is no denying that the boy is beautiful. All thick, black hair and long lashes that women would kill to have. His eyes are such a light blue that they're almost eerie, and for a nineteen-year-old, he is all muscle. Nothing like the scrawny little teenage shits that I went to community college with who thought they were God's gift to women.

Almost painfully shy at first, Aiden has really begun to blossom over the last few months. With Esme's careful guidance, he has started social media accounts for High Tide, and they're already flourishing. Some days, I even wish I could steal him away from her and have him help to establish an online presence for The Grateful Thread, too. And while I haven't had any conversations with him about what his long-term goals are, I know he'd absolutely kill it in social media marketing.

The trio begin talking, Maeve being her animated self while both men hang on her every word, and I take that as my cue to leave. Pushing up from the chair, I collect a few sheets of paper I had been scribbling on before giving Maeve a hug. "I don't know how I would ever be able to pull this off without you."

"It's simple," she replies breezily. "You wouldn't!"

I laugh, knowing that she is right.

Pushing open the front door of Black, White, and Read All Over, I take a second to admire the chalkboard that sits on the sidewalk outside the entrance. Today, it reads, *Treat Yo Shelf* along with several drawings of the spines of books. I often forget to see what the sign de jour is, but when I do remember, I'm never disappointed by the often-hysterical puns and drawings that accompany them.

Sneaking a glance at my phone, I see it's after five in the evening. Still, the sun hangs high in the sky, and I want to take advantage of the last few hours of daylight. Sliding across my phone's home screen, I open my messages and type out a text.

IMOGEN: What are you doing right this second?

ESME: Waiting for this beautiful woman I know to get off work.

I squeal at my phone screen but play along, not letting her know how much her simple words thrill me.

IMOGEN: Oh, maybe I should let you go then. Wouldn't want to tie you up.

ESME: Baby, you know you can tie me up anytime you'd like.

IMOGEN: *GIF of woman fainting*

Okay, so that coolness of mine lasted mere seconds, but what do you expect when she starts talking to me all smooth like that?

IMOGEN: Get a suit on. I'm picking you up in a half hour.

ESME: Bathing suit or a suit of the evening attire?

IMOGEN: Bathing, you silly woman.

IMOGEN: But now that I think of it, you'd look hot as sin in a suit.

ESME: Wishful thinking, beautiful. I don't own one.

IMOGEN: We'll have to change that.

IMOGEN: See you soon!

ESME: Drive safe, sweetheart.

ESME: Love you.

IMOGEN: Not as much as I love you!

I want to scream into the air, want to run to the roof of the plaza and yell to the people walking the sidewalks that I am so incredibly in love with the most amazing woman in the entire world. That I get to call her mine and that she calls me hers in return still baffles me daily. Almost eight billion people on the planet and I get to exist in the same time and space as Esme Galloway.

Thinking that I should probably play the lottery because that's how lucky I am, I duck into my car and tuck my notes into my glove compartment before driving off toward Esme's apartment, all too ready to have her back in my arms for the night.

Thirty-Three
Esme

IN KNEE-DEEP WATER, I HOLD THE EDGES OF THE STAND-UP paddle board, trying my best not to topple back into the calm waters as I work my way into a kneeling position on the rough surface of the board. After taking several calming breaths, I exchange my knees for my feet, slowly pushing myself up and into a standing position.

Next to me, Imogen wrestles with her own board, giggling as she shifts her weight. Centering herself on the board, she kicks her legs further apart, pointing her toes forward.

"The kid at the rental counter said that we should keep our gaze on the horizon and not stare at our feet," she says, standing on her board as if she's done this many times before.

I laugh as I try to keep my balance, my paddle dipping into the water for the first time. "How are you staying so damn still over there? I feel like I'm going to fall in at any second."

Imogen giggles in response, her own paddle connecting with the water in several sweeping strokes, turning her board around and around in circles. "Do you see me, Esme? I keep turning around—definitely not still. I just can't figure out how to move forward!"

Initially apprehensive when Imogen told me to put on a suit, that feeling melted into excitement when we pulled into the small, bayside surf shack. Among surfboards and beach umbrellas, several stand-up paddle boards sat among the equipment available for rent, and I instantly knew that was what Imogen had planned for the evening.

Now, as we both float aimlessly in the calm waters of the bay, I'm not as confident as I was when practicing the motions on dry land.

"Forward strokes!" I call out as I plant my paddle in the water, adjusting my strokes and alternating between the left and right sides of my board.

She gets the hang of it quickly, catching up to me as I glide along the bay. Several kayakers paddle off in the distance, the sun dancing in setting rays across the waters.

It's magical being out here, the quiet sounds of paddles gliding through the water mixed with birds soaring overhead and the occasional laughter from other people enjoying the bay. And when I think it can't get any better, Imogen calls out to me from several feet behind me, "Look to your left, about fifty yards!"

In the distance, a school of dolphins cut through the calm waters, splashing and playing as they dive under the surf before reappearing. Their blue-gray skin reflects the light as water sluices from their bodies with each emergence.

Imogen pulls up next to me on her board, lightly knocking into me by accident. We laugh, both of us nearly falling into the water but managing to regain our composure. For several minutes we watch the dolphins play, barely moving on our boards until a speedboat enters the bay, chasing the creatures off to the deeper waters of the open sea.

The small boat speeds by, its wake reaching out to where we still stand on our boards. While small, the boat packs a powerful punch, and as the small waves it produced hit the edge of our boards, we both topple into the waters, nearly missing one another as we splash into the bay in a fit of giggles.

Our leashes tether us to our boards, preventing them from floating too far. Knowing they can't drift away, I take the opportunity to pull Imogen into my arms as we tread water together. "I'm so fucking in love with you, sweetheart."

She smiles back at me, her hair plastered to her face from the fall. I'm sure mine doesn't look much better, but in all honesty, I never cared about something less in my life. All that matters is me and Imogen and this beautiful life we're building together.

As the sun continues to sink into the sky, ready to be replaced by the moon, we manage to ungracefully slide ourselves back onto our boards after a few failed attempts filled with laughter. Quietly, we paddle back toward shore, awash in the fading oranges and yellows of the setting sun.

We turn in our rentals and head to Imogen's car, our fingers linked together. She walks me to the passenger side, opening the door for me, and in such a small gesture, I feel her love.

Imogen is an expert in showing me that love. It's in the way she truly listens when I talk—like setting up this spur-of-the-moment excursion today, checking off an item from my summer bucket list. It's in her small hand squeezes and gentle caresses, in the way she holds me at night, and the way she pays attention to my body when we're together between the sheets.

Crossing to her side of the car, she slides behind the wheel before turning the key in the ignition, bringing her little red Volkswagen Beetle to life. "My place or yours?"

I'm not sure what prompts it, but instead of answering her question with a response, I answer with a question of my own. "When is your lease up?"

Pulling the car out of the parking space, we sit at the exit, left to her apartment or right to mine. "Three months," she replies, a quizzical crease between her brows.

"Move in with me when it's up."

She gasps, but I keep going. "I know it's soon, and I know it sounds crazy, but I hate this constant back and forth we're doing. I want your clothes in my closet—all of them. I want to carpool on days we work at the same time and cook you dinner at night in my kitchen—in *our* kitchen. Let's find a place together—a place we can call ours."

Her eyes are full of moisture as she looks at me. "I want all of that, too. More than you'll ever know!"

"Is that a yes?"

"Of course, it's a yes!"

We stare at each other, both smiling with big, goofy grins on our faces.

I know my abs are going to be sore tomorrow from standing up on the paddle board for hours, but now, I'm confident my cheeks are going to ache just as much from the smile on my face.

A horn honks behind us, breaking us out of our love-filled daze. Quickly, Imogen looks to her left, then right, before finally turning right, taking us back to my apartment and toward what awaits.

"What about you?" she asks when we're stepping into my small shower together a short time later, ready to wash the salt water from our skin.

Taking a loofa from a small hook, I pour some body wash onto the poof before working it into a thick lather. I run it over Imogen's back, loving that she gives me this small moment of intimacy where I care for her in such a gentle way. "What about me?" I respond, unsure of what she means.

"When is your lease up? I don't want to put you into an uncomfortable position with the Farleys."

Imogen turns toward me, allowing me to run the sponge over the front of her body. I lather her neck and shoulders, sliding down over her chest, under each breast, and over her stomach. "I'm on a month-to-month basis with them." Moving further down her body, I crouch to soap up each leg before running the sponge up between her legs.

I slide my hands over the loofa, collecting soap and suds

between my fingers. Then, I drop the sponge and slide my hands between her legs, relishing in the gasp that leaves her mouth.

Slowly, I work between her legs, the soap making her already responsive body even slicker. "I'm going to miss this place," Imogen says with a gasp as I brush against her clit. "Going to miss our walks to the atoll, miss the way the mattress squeaks when we roll around on top of it…" She groans as I remove my hand, making quick work of rinsing her body.

"Not going to miss the way we always run out of hot water before we're done in here, are you?" I tell her as the water temperature turns from tepid to frigid.

She laughs, jumping out of the shower and quickly wrapping herself in an oversized towel. Under the cold water, I wash in haste, finishing up as fast as I can. It's only partially because of the water temperature, the rest of my rush coming only from wanting to be next to Imogen again.

Her body is splayed across my mattress when I exit the bathroom a short time later. Propped against a pillow, her wet hair hangs around her shoulders, still dripping onto her skin. The tiny beads of water roll down her body and over her chest, and while goosebumps have spread across most of her skin, she makes no move to cover herself.

Instead, Imogen brings her hands up to the water droplets, rubbing them over her skin before skating her hands down her torso. One hand dips between her legs, teasing between her bare folds.

Part of me wants her to stop, wants to be the only hands that ever touch her in such an intimate way. Yet there is a small, primal side somewhere deep inside of me, coaxing her to continue, wanting to simply stand at the edge of the bed as she fucks herself under my watchful gaze.

I watch with rapt attention for several moments as she continues to tease herself, her eyes boring into my soul the entire time. Stepping closer to the bed, she holds up her other hand, silently telling me to stop where I'm at.

"Take off your towel," she tells me in a commanding voice I'm unused to hearing from her.

While Imogen and I don't have any set dynamic, in the past, I have taken control when we're together. Tonight, she's holding the reins, and I absolutely do not hate it. Seeing her touch herself was already a turn-on, but when she speaks those words to me in such a low, smooth voice, the wetness between my thighs grows.

The towel flutters to the floor around me as I follow her instructions, watching as her eyes appreciatively rake over my own body.

"I don't tell you enough how beautiful you are," she says as she pushes herself up to her knees. "Come here and kneel in front of me."

Obeying her commands, I make my way onto the mattress, imitating her position while leaving only a few inches between us. With one hand still between her own legs, her other cups my breast before her fingers lightly pinch my already peaked nipple.

Imogen leans into me, capturing my lips with her own. She bites my bottom lip, eliciting a groan in response, and when the hand that was previously between her thighs slides between mine with one efficient stroke, I almost come apart at the seams.

"Jesus Christ, sweetheart," I tell her through gritted teeth.

Her low, almost sadistic chuckle is all I need to hear to know that she's fully aware of the effect she is having on my body.

Without toppling us, Imogen manages to come closer, her thighs straddling one of my own as she continues to work her fingers through my folds. She circles my clit, dragging my slickness from my cunt up to tease me.

Her second arm steadies us as she rests it on my shoulder, slowly rocking her hips over my naked thigh with cautious movements. "You have no idea how much I love you," she moans. "How hard it is to keep my hands off you for even a minute."

Sliding her fingers away from my clit, she moves them lower and lower until she's sliding two fingers deep inside my pussy. Her hips rock back and forth over my leg, and I can feel the slick moisture of her arousal as she grinds against me. "More," I rasp out. "Give me more."

She gives me more of both pleasure and words, adding another two fingers to my cunt, stretching me even further. It burns in a painfully wonderful way, and while I've never felt so full as I do right now, I know in this moment that one day, I want to take all of that hand deep inside my cunt.

I somehow manage to sneak one of my own hands between my body and hers, finding her clit and rolling it between my fingers. "God, yes!" she moans. "I'm so close, Esme. So close!"

"Me too, baby," I tell her, dropping my forehead to hers. "Can you come with me baby? Let me see you soak my thigh. Show me how wet you can leave me."

Imogen's hips thrust faster and faster as she grinds herself against me, all the while her fingers keep up a frantic pace, spearing me deep. Curling them deep within, she hits a sacred spot that has my pussy clenching around her digits. Her hand that has been balancing us on my shoulder tangles in my hair, a forceful tug exposing my neck.

With that tug, I explode, bucking my own hips in time, clenching around Imogen's fingers with even more force. Seconds later, she is following me, wetness leaking from her pretty pussy to coat my thigh as she continues to writhe on both my leg and hand.

Her lips come down to meet the sensitive spot where my neck and shoulder meet, and she sucks at my skin, enough that I'm sure she's left a mark.

Let her mark me, I think to myself. *Let her show the world that I am hers.*

"Yours, Immy," I tell her, breathlessly panting as the stars from behind my eyelids dissipate.

"Yours," she repeats, pulling me down onto the mattress, curling her body around mine on instinct before we drift off to sleep, while I begin the countdown until we move in together, truly the start of our forever.

Thirty-Four

Luna Sea Plaza
Owner's Chat

SUNDAY: If I have to watch one more episode of this damn dog with an Australian accent, I'm going to fucking scream.

SUNDAY: Please tell me you're all free on Saturday night. I need to be around adults desperately.

OAKEN: Could be worse.

OAKEN: Could be that little bald asshole kid instead.

MAEVE: OMG, Oaken! You shouldn't talk about kids like that!

CAMPBELL: I believe he is referring to Caillou, the animated children's character.

OAKEN: Punk ass.

CAMPBELL: What the hell, man.

OAKEN: Not you, dude. The cartoon kid.

OAKEN: Total punk ass.

HOLLIS: Oh, come on, we all know Cammy is a punk ass, too.

ESME: I'm staying out of this conversation.

IMOGEN: But we are free on Saturday!

OAKEN: Same here.

SUNDAY: Maeve? Hollis?

MAEVE: I'll check what my man has planned and get back to you.

HOLLIS: Which man?

WATSON: AM I INVITED OR AM I TOO OLD?

OAKEN: Oh, Lord, here we go with the caps lock again.

Thirty-Five
Imogen

FROM ACROSS THE ROOM, I STARE AT ESME WHERE SHE STANDS on a small stool in the back room of The Grateful Thread. On the floor in front of her, Grandma Birdie crouches, a pin cushion strapped to one wrist. With several pins tucked between her teeth, she slowly rotates around Esme, placing a few pins through the fabric of what will soon be Esme's finished, custom-tailored suit.

And it couldn't have come at a better time.

In my hand, my phone vibrates, and I have to stifle a laugh at the message from Sunday.

SUNDAY: Hope that was good enough! Thought playing it off as needing an adult-only night would get her to take the bait!

IMOGEN: Worked like a charm! She has no idea!

I sneak a quick picture as final pins are placed and send the photo off to Sunday. A few minutes later, my phone vibrates again. While Maeve has helped with the majority of the planning for our prom, both Sunday and Hollis have been in on the action, too. Even Oaken has stepped in a few times, secretly loving his position as one of the unofficial party planners.

SUNDAY: Dayummm, girl! Look how hot your woman looks!

IMOGEN: Don't get any ideas. She's all mine!

SUNDAY: Good thing I already have my hands full. *Wink emoji*

I respond with a laugh and pocket my phone, turning my

attention back to the beautiful woman placed on a pedestal where she rightfully belongs.

With just a few final alterations, Esme's suit is going to fit her like a glove. The black pants are slim fitting, showing off her frame, while a fitted, matching, black, three-button vest completes the look. I can't wait to see her on the night of the dance, all dressed for the occasion, and even splurged to find her an amazing shirt and tie to top off the ensemble.

Esme is always beautiful with her carefree style and mussed hair, but today, seeing her in this suit has my insides acting all fuzzy. She looks more androgynous in this suit, like a sexy runway model off the hottest fashion-week show, and I can already picture how she could wear this look while dressed up for a night on the town or more casual with an oversized hat and slouchy purse looped over her shoulder.

I must be staring because before I realize it, Esme is back in front of me in her street clothes. Placing a kiss against my lips, we part ways as she heads for the High Tide store.

"Oh, my beautiful grandchild, you've got it bad, don't you?" Though Birdie says the words in jest, she already knows that she is spot on.

I sigh into the quiet backroom like a lovesick, little puppy. "I know it has been close to seven months since she's been back, but sometimes, I still think it's all just too good to be true. I still worry about her disappearing into thin air. Just like last time."

Birdie gives me a gentle little pat, as if I've never grown up from the small child she taught how to quilt all those years ago. "You made it through a decade of distance, sweet girl. I've seen the way she looks at you and how you look at her, and there is no doubt in my mind that you both have what it takes to go the distance. You stood by her through everything when a lesser woman may have felt her baggage was too much."

My grandmother pulls me into a reassuring hug. "But not you. You've shown her time and time again that you are here as her partner and that you not only want to be at her side, but you want to help to lessen her burden, too. You've taken on that baggage as your own, shared in her joys and her sorrows. And that, dear Imogen, is what a partnership is about."

So overcome with emotion, I begin to cry, still cradled in the gentle arms of my grandmother. "She asked me to move in with her when my lease is up. We're going to try to find a place together."

She strokes my back with weathered hands, a gentle rhythm that reminds me of a mother caring for a newborn. "I bet you're excited about that, aren't you?"

"Very," I tell her earnestly. "I know it will come with challenges, but you're right, Grandma. Whatever comes our way, we'll be able to overcome it together."

"Damn right, kiddo." She gives me a final squeeze before pushing me from the back room. "Now get out there and help our customers. This place isn't going to run itself."

I'm barely at work for three hours when Esme enters the shop once again. I look up to find her in the doorway, a smile tipping up the corner of her lips. When our eyes lock, the smile widens, her dimples appearing in the corner of her cheeks. Finishing up with the customer I had been ringing up, I then cross the store to where she stands next to a pile of colorful fabric remnants on sale.

"Can you take five?" she asks. "I have something to tell you!"

From her apparent excitement, I'm happy that whatever she has to share seems like it will be positive. I look around the store at the few customers milling about. I'm about to tell her whatever she has to tell me will have to wait until later when Allison shouts from across the room, "Go ahead! Get out of here. We've got it!"

We walk through the back of the store and make our way to the small picnic table in the back of the plaza. Sitting next to one another on the bench, Esme takes my hand in hers before turning to fully face me.

Her energy is palpable, and it's making me more excited for whatever she has to tell me.

"I spoke with the Farleys today about our plans, about us moving in together when your lease is up."

Some of my excitement begins to fade. I know it couldn't have been an easy conversation to have with her school-librarian-turned-landlord-turned-friend. "You're way too excited for someone who had to deliver shitty news."

Esme raises her eyebrows in a suggestive yet playful nature. "That's where you're wrong, my love. You see, when I chatted with Anita on the phone this afternoon, she offered up a very unique proposal."

The gears in my brain are moving, but I can't come up with any proposal that would be beneficial for both the Farleys and Esme. "Are you going to keep me guessing, or are you going to tell me?" I ask on a huff.

Pulling me across the bench, Esme brings me closer to her body, placing a quick kiss on the tip of my nose. "You're extra cute when you're impatient."

I swat her away, but she resists. "What if I told you that the Farleys were already talking about downsizing?"

A bit of the tension drains from my shoulders. "That's great news! So, they won't mind losing you as a renter?"

She nods in response, while continuing to speak. "They won't mind losing me as a renter, *and* they've offered to sell the house to us and will only put it up on the market if we decide to go in a different direction."

My mouth hangs open in surprise, thinking about the Farleys' beautiful house. I picture the gorgeous porch with the rocking chairs that sit side-by-side, the overflowing planters that bring color to the front of the house year after year. I think of the back-yard with its small garden and fragrant pergola that covers a tiny, brick porch. And then, I think of the pathway in the brush, the sandy trail that leads over land until...

"The atoll," I say, a hitch in my voice.

Esme brings her gorgeously calloused hands to my face, cupping my cheeks on either side. Lightly, she brushes her thumbs under my eyes in a tender and intimate moment. "It's part of their private land, the reason why we could never find it as kids. But Immy, sweetheart, it could be ours now."

In the months since she has been back, she has only called me Immy a handful of times. Yet each time she has used my childhood nickname, it signifies something important, and this conversation is no different.

Already, I can see us living in the Farleys' house—*our* house. Hosting parties and game nights with our friends, holidays and birthdays with my family crowded around a large, dining room table. My mind flashes with nights spent on the sandy atoll, days spent sharing sweet tea on the front porch as we watch summer storms roll across the sky, and I can already pick out more than one place inside the large foyer perfect for a live Christmas Tree complete with no less than a million multi-colored lights.

"I want it," I tell her on an exhale, the air whooshing out of my lungs as I think of all the possibilities. "I want to build a life with you in that house. I want to start our forever there, where we've already created so many special memories."

Esme's smile is wide, her eyes glistening with approbation as she pulls me closer and closer until I'm straddling her lap in broad daylight, the hem of my dress offering us a small amount of decency as it bunches up around us.

I silently pray to God that a heavy gust of wind doesn't blow up the back of my dress, showing off my bare ass to anyone who decides to walk or drive by while Esme wraps her arms around me. "God, I was worried you would think it was a horrible idea. That you would think I was crazy, but baby, I feel the same exact way. It's where we belong, where we can grow and expand our family."

Esme must sense the panic that flashes in my eyes because she quickly corrects herself. "No, no, no. Not kids—no way. But maybe a dog or two. Maybe Taylor Swift could have a permanent home. Or we could rescue one from the shelter. We could continue to rent out the apartment over the garage at a super affordable rate. Maybe to someone from the community who is a little down on their luck and needs a temporary home, maybe to a LGBTQ+ teen who is escaping a bad family life like I had."

The smile is back on my face, everything she says exactly the same as what first ran through my head. "Yes, I want that. I want all of that with you, and I want it in that house. Tell me what we have to do to make it happen, and I'm there."

We share several long kisses, smiling into each other with each press of our lips. I pull away, needing to put space between us before we take this celebration to the next level—something completely inappropriate in broad daylight.

"Go and call Anita," I tell her as I push up from the picnic table. "I've got to get back inside before Allison and Birdie level the store to the ground."

When I turn to walk away, she pulls me back into her once more, placing a big, sloppy kiss full of so much emotion right across my lips.

"To the future, sweetheart," she tells me.

I shake my head at her as I walk away. "No, Esme. To *our* future."

Thirty-Six
Esme

Another Saturday night is upon us, and while I'm used to hanging out with a bunch of members of the plaza at this point, I'm not used to being in anything more than jeans and a t-shirt at our often impromptu get-togethers.

Tonight though, Imogen instructed me to wear my newest outfit, a custom-tailored Grandma Birdie exclusive suit. The black fabric accentuates what little curves I have, making me feel slightly less like a teenage boy than normal. Beneath the black, button-up vest, I have on a bubblegum-pink shirt, rolled up a few times because hello, Florida heat. The shirt, a gift from Imogen earlier this week, makes my skin look even tanner than it is, and the matching tie in a paisley pattern so closely mimics pieces of our quilt that I wonder if it is from the same fabric.

I have no idea what our plans are with our friends, Imogen insisting that she knew all the details when I asked in our group chat. But I know it's going to be different than our normal dive bar where we play trivia or sing so badly at karaoke night that we get booed off the stage during a thrilling rendition of Sara Bareilles's *She Used To Be Mine*.

Slipping my feet into my dress shoes, I take one last look in the mirror, admiring the way I look. My hair is as unruly as ever, growing slightly longer over the last few months, yet I like the way it looks now that it is almost brushing my shoulders. With a constant place to call home—some semblance of normalcy—

I've put on some weight, the deep hollows under my eyes finally seeming to disappear, a long-gone reminder of my previous life.

Honking in the driveway below catches my attention and without a glance backwards, I grab my wallet and phone, tucking them into the extra deep pockets of my suit pants—one of the only requests I had for my outfit.

Expecting to see Imogen's little, red Bug, I'm surprised to see a large, black bus in the driveway. Confused, I approach, ready to talk to the driver, but am stunned into silence as the door opens and members of my team exit the bus, each one dressed just as fancy, if not fancier, than I am.

Aiden and Zander hold out their hands, each taking a turn to do a silly spin.

"What do you think, boss?" Zander asks. "We clean up nicely, don't we?"

Aveline pulls me into a hug. "Woman, you absolutely rock that look. Now let's go!"

Still unsure of what is happening, I try to speak but am cut off, this time by Aiden. "Don't worry. Your special lady is waiting for you at our secret destination. Get on the bus and we'll be there in no time."

Heeding their instructions, I step onto the bus, laughing at the interior. Fitted with couches all around the perimeter of the bus, the ceiling is mirrored, and an honest to goodness stripper pole sits in the middle of the space. There is more than one ice bucket perched on top of built-in tables, and I spot bottles of beer as well as individual-serving-sized bottles of champagne among various other drinks and snacks. In all, there is probably space for at least fifteen adults inside the interior of the bus. It conjures images in my mind of what it would have been like to attend my senior prom with Imogen by my side—minus the champagne and beer, of course.

I take a seat, my friends crowding around me to fill in the

space, and then, we're off. Only when someone calls to the front of the bus do I take note of our driver.

"Watson!" I call out to the old man, equally dressed to the nines. "How did you get talked into being our driver for the night?"

"Hello, Esme. Tonight, we're on a need-to-know basis and that's something you don't need to know. Now relax and enjoy the entertainment on the way to our destination."

He shoots me a wink before he slams a button on the dashboard, allowing music to fill the air of the bus. Aveline twirls around on the pole, not really performing, but using it as a prop as she sings along to the music. Eileen and Sarah sit on benches off to one side, while Zander and Aiden sit across the bus on the other. Stretching across the back of the bus, Ezra sits like a king, arms outstretched to either side. His khaki pants pull tightly across his thick thighs while equally as solid biceps nearly tear through his white dress shirt. It sometimes surprises me that the man is still single, looking like a freaking Greek sculpture come to life.

Our bus twists and turns as we make our way through downtown Luna Harbor, and for the life of me, I cannot imagine where we are going. As a new song begins to play over the sound system, we pass the playground for the third time, and I begin to grow even more suspicious.

"Where are we going?" I ask Aveline as she sits, leaving the pole open for Zander to playfully twirl around. I'm only half-focused on her response, my attention rapt as I watch his large form undulate against the metal with more grace than I would expect him to have.

Eileen lets out a wolf whistle, the eldest of our group of employees enjoying the impromptu dance from one of our two youngest. Pulling a dollar from somewhere between her breasts, she tucks it into the waistband of Zander's pants while the rest of the bus erupts into a chorus of applause.

"If you're lucky, maybe I'll show you even more at the after-party!" he teases, tossing a saucy wink in the direction of Eileen, who flushes pink.

Again, I try to get Aveline's attention. "After-party?"

She brushes me aside again, handing me a miniature bottle of champagne and changing the subject. "Drink up, beautiful. It's going to be one hell of a wild night!"

Giving into the swirling excitement buzzing around the party bus, I tilt the bottle to my lips, taking a long pull from the cold, glass bottle. Aveline squeals, holding her own bottle to mine. We clink them together in celebration as we pull into the parking lot of the local high school. My emotions have been a hurricane of back and forths since the time I began getting ready today that I'm nearly certain I have whiplash at this point. "What are we doing at the school?"

"Don't move a muscle," Aveline responds, jumping up from where she was seated next to me. She is through the bus and out the door before I have a chance to ask her again what the hell is going on.

One by one, the rest of my employees-turned-friends leave the bus until it's just me and Watson. Slowly, Watson pushes open the driver's side door. Before climbing out and shutting the door, he turns around to face me where I am sitting in the rear of the party bus. Taking my hand in his, he slips a gorgeous floral corsage over my wrist, the leaves and petals tickling my skin. "Enjoy every moment of your night, Esme. You deserve it, dear."

And just like that, I'm sitting alone on the bus. Quiet music still playing, sad stripper pole sitting by its lonesome in the middle of the bus, just waiting for a sweaty body to grind up against it like a teenager in a sweaty high school gym on prom night.

Starting to wonder if my friends are all playing some sort of odd prank on me, I stand, determined to reach the door to see what is happening behind the shiny interior of the party bus.

But before I make it more than a few feet, the door to the bus opens, and my breath catches in my throat, leaving me utterly speechless.

Imogen ascends the stairs, standing in front of me in a bubblegum-pink dress, the very shade of my shirt. Nearly identical to the one she wore at the long-ago ill-fated dance, thin straps hold up the dress while a thigh-high slit runs up her left leg. The bodice is covered in crystals, and she shimmers in the low lights of the bus. Tonight, her usual casual hair is styled into gorgeous, loose waves that hang down around her shoulders. Smoky shadow has been swiped across her lids, her cheeks a rosy pink. Nude gloss coats her lips, and despite the slickness of its appearance, I lean forward and take her lips in mine.

"I have absolutely no idea what we're doing here, no idea what evil plan you have concocted, but before you tell me anything, I have to tell you how fucking gorgeous you look, Immy."

Imogen gives me a small smile in return, sliding her hands into mine. She smells like coconut and peaches tonight, a combination that makes me think of endless summers and daiquiris while sitting on the hot sand. "I could say the very same thing about you. I knew you'd look amazing in a tailored suit. Now come on, Esme. We have a few dances to make up for."

With eager steps, I follow her down the steps of the bus, my eyes going wide when I take in the crew that has gathered in the parking lot.

Along with all my staff, Grandma Birdie and Allison from The Grateful Thread are here, alongside all the store owners from the plaza. Even Campbell is nearby, dressed in an impeccable three-piece suit. I make out Asher, now off to the side chatting with Zander, and see Aiden blushing from between Maeve and her husband, Sebastian.

I turn to Imogen, full of bewilderment and in awe of the woman in front of me. She holds out her hand, which I willingly take, intertwining our fingers together tightly. All around us, our friends snap pictures and laugh, and in the distance, I hear music coming from the direction of the school's gymnasium.

"If it's too much, if it's too soon, we don't have to go inside. But there is something extra special happening in there tonight in your honor, and I think you're going to love it."

I tighten my grip on her hand, inhaling and exhaling a few deep, calming breaths.

"You ready?" she asks, just low enough for me to hear over the rumble of our friends.

Never expecting to walk back into the halls of this place again, I hesitate for only a second before walking toward the entrance, our entire crew in tow behind us. Expecting to feel a wash of anxiousness, I'm surprised when instead, I feel nothing but peace and excitement. "Yeah, baby, I'm ready."

Thirty-Seven
Imogen

WALKING INTO THE HIGH SCHOOL GYMNASIUM WITH ESME ON MY arm is a surreal experience. Sure, we attended one dance together as teens, but not like this. Not with our fingers linked together and huge smiles on our faces, not together as an out-and-proud couple who don't have to hide from our peers and family.

It's the most amazing moment of my life.

The way in which Maeve was able to work with local companies to transform the gym completely blew me away when I first stepped inside tonight, and now, I'm in awe again as I take in the space through Esme's view.

Tables are scattered throughout the room, flanking a large, wooden dance floor. A live band has already begun playing on stage, a mix of current pop hits and songs from our youth on a constant loop. Purple and silver linens adorn each table in a not-so-subtle nod to our school, while the rest of the room is blanketed under a riot of rainbow colors. Paper lanterns hang from the ceiling, giving the space an overall glow. Interspersed with the lanterns, shiny silver stars hang at different heights, each with the name of one of the teens who is here tonight. A subtle nod to let each and every one of them know that they can be the star of their own life, they'll be able to take their star home at the end of the night as a reminder of their prom experience.

Several large balloon arches stand proudly in the room. A photographer stands off to the side of one, waiting to capture groups and couples in cliché prom poses that will undoubtedly stand the test of time.

Atop a nearby table, a fountain trickles a signature non-alcoholic drink while two ice sculptures flank either side. The first sculpture is two interconnected hearts done in the colors of the original pride flag, while the second spells out the words *Love is Love* in a gorgeous script. I wouldn't be able to copy the script of the words, even if I was copying them onto a piece of paper. Truly, some people have no limits to their talents.

Each table has endless swag in the forms of glow sticks, Pride flags, bottles of bubbles, and temporary tattoos, while several dress-up stations around the room have everything from sunglasses and top hats to feather boas and tiaras.

Esme's eyes are comically wide as they bounce around the room for a solid minute before she finally turns back to me. "You…you did all of this for me?"

Her beautiful voice is heavy with emotion, tightening my chest with her sincerity. While she is still as confident as I always remember her to be, her self-worth seemed so broken, almost shattered, when she first came back to Luna Harbor all those months ago. Esme has finally started to see that she is worthy of love, and I can't wait to show her that love every day for the rest of our lives.

Several of our friends are already out on the dance floor, dancing and singing as the music moves through the room. Pulling Esme into my arms, I hug her tightly to my chest. "I did it for you. For us. But also, for all of them."

I turn us back toward the entrance of the gym, a different door than we entered through, allowing Esme to see the teens as they begin to pour into the room. Their faces light up as they take in the space, naturally gravitating toward photo backdrops and the dance floor.

In total, almost two hundred teens are here in all manner of dress, some traveling from up to three hours away for the experience. As I cast my gaze across the room, I take in floor-length gowns and cocktail dresses, khaki pants and three-piece suits. Many have already begun adding accessories from the tables, a few feathers in various colors floating across the gym from boas that have been snatched up and wrapped around bodies.

"What is all of this?" Esme asks after taking in everything happening around us. The energy is frenetic and wild, the music growing louder as more and more teens take to the dance floor.

Walking Esme toward the photographer, we hop in line to have our pictures taken while I tell her more about the event that everyone from Luna Sea Plaza had a hand in helping to organize.

"I wanted to do something special for you, to show you that your past doesn't define you. I thought if you could replace that first dance with this one, that maybe it would help to lessen the pain—even just a menial amount—and it would give you something good to think about when you see the school or think back on school dances."

Her eyes are misty, and I have to laugh, thinking back to all the times we've cried or teared up in front of each other since she moved back to town. And while many of those tears have been tears of pain and longing, so many more have been tears of love and happiness. The kind of tears that appear without warning when emotion takes hold, and we are at a loss of words.

Esme swipes at her cheeks, wiping away the few tears that managed to sneak past her attempts to contain them. I can't stop myself from leaning in to press a kiss to her temple when she asks, "Who are all these kids?"

"It felt selfish to do all of this just for us. I know what you went through, and I know that there are many other kids just like you—just like *us*. I wanted to include them in a prom where they could be fully in their element. No school administrators telling them that they can't bring a same-sex partner, no one to tell them that they can't wear a dress because they are male or a tux because they are female."

Just then, Lady Gaga's *Born This Way* begins to blast over the speakers, the live band fully playing to their audience as the teens—and Grandma Birdie—begin to sing along at the top of their lungs. She grabs Watson's hand, pulling him toward the dance floor, throwing a saucy wave in our direction that has us erupting into a fit of side-splitting laughter.

"Shit on a shingle," Esme says. "I don't think Watson knows what he's gotten himself into."

"None of us ever do when it comes to that woman," I tell her in response.

As the couple in front of us, two teenagers in near-matching purple dresses, take their spot in front of the camera, I can't help but stare at them. They can't be more than fourteen, and it reminds me so much of Esme and myself at that age. Although by their close contact, they feel comfortable enough to not shield away from other eyes in the gym, unlike we had to do nearly a decade ago.

Esme must notice the similarities, too, resting her chin on my shoulder as she wraps her arms around me from behind. "This is fucking magical, sweetheart. How long have you been planning this?"

I lean into her touch, exhaling on a sigh, simply never wanting to leave her safe embrace. "Since the night you told me your truth. It just…it wasn't fair back then, and it isn't fair now."

We approach the marked spot under the rainbow arch of balloons, the photographer walking us through several traditional prom poses. Esme behind me with her arms around my waist, me repeating the pose behind her. The photographer captures us hugging and laughing before snapping his last photo—one where Esme leans in and presses her lips to mine.

The entire night we dance and sing, take breaks to sip on the super sugary punch, and enjoy the company of our friends and teens around us. Several of the kids approach me, thanking me for hosting the event, and I make it a point to tell each one that it was a group effort and that it never would have happened without the woman next to me.

Finally having a chance to sit, I kick off my heels under the table and stretch out my feet. Maeve is next to me, prattling on about the success of the night, and I can't help but feel immense joy as I watch Esme laughing and dancing with Grandma Birdie to the *Cupid Shuffle*.

"You really should be proud of yourself, Imogen," the bookstore owner says without looking at me. Following her line of sight, I see Sebastian on the floor, Aiden next to him as the pair also participate in the almost ludicrous line dance.

I smile because I *am* proud. But it isn't the pride I feel from putting an event together that makes me smile; it's the pride I feel in being able to do something for so many of my friends and teens that otherwise may not have been given the opportunity to experience something full of so much magic. The pride I feel in celebrating my love with Esme and the pride I feel simply by standing at her side.

The music shifts into a slower song, and Aiden and Esme approach the table. As Esme holds out a hand to me, Aiden does the same, only gesturing for Maeve to take his outstretched hand.

We take our place on the dance floor, my arms coming to loop around Esme's neck as she rests hers on my lower back. Together, we sway to the music, taking in everyone dancing around us. Two older boys stand closely together, a red feathered boa circling their upper bodies, they whisper into each other's ears, while a pair of young girls tentatively sway on the opposite side of the room. I point them out to Esme, and she turns to see them, just as their lips ever so gently press against each other.

She pulls me a little closer, holding me as if she's afraid I'll disappear if she lets go. "So young and unaware of everything out in the world. I hope they never feel unwanted, never feel unloved."

My heart clenches in my chest, a small sprig of sadness

trying to bloom into something larger. But I push it back down, wanting only to focus on the good of the night. On the good of having Esme back in my life.

"We'll make sure they feel as much love as the world has to offer," I tell her. "We can volunteer with local organizations if that is something you would like to do. I would gladly go with you. We can be there for them as role models, and even more importantly, as friends. I can host a sewing class for them, teach them about creating their own sense of fashion and style. You could teach the older teens about your industry and all the benefits cannabis can provide. Maybe we can organize a joint beach clean-up where we can get some of the kids to come help.

"I know it doesn't change what happened to you, and I know it is something that you'll always hold on to, but it doesn't mean we can't take those feelings and transfer them into something positive. I mean, just look around us."

Esme holds me tight as she does just that. She scans the gymnasium, looking at the groups and couples on the dance floor. She watches as even more people take pictures while others sit around tables, laughing and joking with one another.

Finally, after a long pause, she replies, "Be the change you wish to see in the world and all that bullshit, right?"

I laugh, but the sound comes out a little hollow. "Quoting Gandhi? Have you been hanging out at Magical, Mystical, Mayhem too much?"

Over the sound of the music, I'm unable to hear her sigh, but I feel it against my body. "It's just a lot of responsibility, you know. To have this desire to mentor and provide a safe space when it isn't something I ever had myself."

Holding her against me with one arm, I use the other to push away some of her unruly curls. "That's what makes you the perfect person to do it. You know more than any of us the resilience it takes to make it through the teen years. What it means to feel like you have to fit in when all you want to do is stand out and speak your truth. Just promise me you'll think about it because you can change the world, Esme. You were *made* to change it."

Over the mic, one of the band's singers announces the last song of the evening and invites everyone to join those of us still on the dance floor. All around us, our friends from the plaza surround our space. Birdie wraps her arms around both of us, singing along to Journey's *Don't Stop Believin'*, Aiden sways to the song, his arm stretched over Sebastian's shoulder. Even Campbell stands on the floor, though his hands remain in his pockets.

The song finishes to a chorus of shouts and cheers, of whistles and screams. Friends, both old and new, snap last-minute pictures before grabbing as many items off the tables as they can. Good riddance to the colorful accessories; it's just one last thing to clean up.

I must give out fifty hugs to teens on their way out, an ongoing slew of thank you's and please do this again next year's. Looking for Esme, I see the same is happening to her from her place across the gym. And with each hug she receives, with each high five and handshake and selfie she poses for, her smile grows wider and wider, the words of affirmation she's receiving enough to push her into knowing she too can make a difference.

She's already made a huge difference to me.

Thirty-Eight
Esme

As much as I enjoyed my time living and learning in Colorado, the beach will always be my home. It truly has a way of cleansing my soul, of making me feel just a little lighter. Tonight, as I sit on the beach surrounded by friends who laugh and sing, I don't just feel like my soul has been cleansed; I feel reborn, a daring phoenix about to rise from the ashes.

After the Luna Harbor LGBTQIA+ Prom ended, we all piled into the party bus, getting a head start on the after-party while Watson drove us toward the beach. This time, Grandma Birdie sat in the passenger seat while several others, including Sunday and Campbell, joined us on the bus.

Now, we've all changed into more appropriate beach attire, and the after-party has really started as several joints are passed around the growing bonfire. Our laughter nearly drowns out the sounds of the waves as they crash along the shoreline.

Imogen has been floating around the fire, soaking in the praise from her friends, and it's so well deserved that I can't help but feel my heart clench in my chest. Not only did she pull off the surprise of the century for me, but she helped to change and shape so many hearts in the process. She gets passed around the fire more than the joint between my fingers, and while I'm anxious to have some much-deserved one-on-one time with my special woman, I'm equally as excited to watch from afar as everyone fusses over how wonderful she is.

I take a moment to reflect on the night, excusing myself from the crowd and making my way to where the water meets the sand. Lowering myself to the ground, I sink into the damp sand, my toes just barely getting brushed by the water with each wave that comes ashore.

In the distance, I can still hear the gentle playing of a guitar, courtesy of Imogen's father, who helped to set up our after-party along with Imogen's mom. The music plinks through the breeze as the laughter and low sounds of conversation drift around me, yet I tune it all out as I turn my head skyward and take in the dark expanse of sky dotted with thousands of stars.

For years of my life, I blamed God for what had happened to me just as much as I blamed my family. I blamed Him for the hate and abuse I experienced at the hands of two of His followers, at the hands of the two very people who were supposed to keep me safe. But now, after everything the last few months have taught me, I find that the blame I placed unfairly on Him has begun to dissipate, and in its place, I feel appreciation and understanding of the complications of being a queer woman. And those are feelings I'm certain I never would have learned to accept had I not ended up back in Luna Harbor.

Yet still, I don't think I'll find myself back in a church environment anytime soon, and that's something I'm still coming to terms with after it being such a staple of my childhood. Honestly, it's a place I may never venture inside again—even the thought of the experience dragging up way more emotion inside than I felt walking back into Luna Harbor High tonight. However, knowing that I'm allowed to be spiritual without being religious is yet another weight that has been lifted off my chest and gives me a small sense of peace.

Briefly, I wonder if Magical Mystical Mayhem would have anything to help me along this newest part of my journey toward fully healing. I turn to seek out Sunday but am left with a sly smile on my face as I make out her and Campbell's forms leaving the beach hand-in-hand.

Turning back to the wide expanse of ocean in front of me, I continue to let the waves tickle my toes, wiggling them in the wet sand. Only a few minutes pass before I feel a presence at my side, and before I can turn to look, Imogen sits in the sand on my right side, her hand gently tipping to rest on my shoulder.

"So, how was your first prom experience?" she asks quietly.

I look down at her from the corner of my eye, her face relaxed as she looks up at the stars, a small smile across her lips.

Reaching out on instinct, I link our fingers together, always feeling better—more grounded—when her hand is in mine. "It was everything I never knew I missed and more. Being with all those kids, seeing how open and free they all are, it was inspiring."

"What I hear you saying is that you want to do it again next year?" she asks hopefully.

Laughing, I manage to pull her a little closer to my side as a wave crests closer to the shore, splashing us up to our thighs. "With you by my side, we'll do it all."

"Starting by sleeping under the stars with me tonight?" Imogen twirls a ring of keys around her finger that I recognize as the keys to the lifeguard stand we set up our party beside. Thanks to Watson and Sure Lock Homes, we have access to the tower for our monthly beach clean-up days, and we keep a few essentials, including beach chairs and blankets, locked in the tower when not in use.

Knowing how excited I was to try paddle boarding, I know Immy is just as excited to check this item off her bucket list, and I'm more than happy to sleep under the stars any night if it keeps the radiant smile on her face that she is giving me now.

When we stand a short time later, it's only then that I realize everyone else has already left, the fire now mere embers a short distance away. There is no sign of the party bus or our friends, and I wonder briefly how they all snuck away without me noticing.

Then again, I tend to lose track of time when Imogen is involved.

Together, we make our way to the lifeguard tower where Imogen ushers me up the four wooden steps that lead to the platform the tower is built upon. The normal slatted, wooden floor is covered by an air mattress and piles upon piles of blankets and pillows. An electric lantern sits nearby, and a small table is set with a chilled bottle of champagne, chocolate-covered strawberries, and a single rose tucked into a bud vase.

Upon closer inspection I laugh, picking up the vase—which is, in actuality, a small bong—and hold it out to Imogen. She simply shrugs in response. "Birdie helped me set things up. What do you expect?"

"It's perfect," I tell her as I set the vase back on the table. "It's all perfect."

She leads me to a small hose that is attached to the side of the lifeguard stand, and we take turns rinsing off our feet and legs, ridding our bodies of leftover sand. Pushing open the door to the small tower, we enter and change into two pairs of brand-new pajamas. Imogen dons a slip-like dress that smooths over her curves and shows off skin, a cheetah print all over the silky material with a small strip of see through lace along the bottom hem.

I laugh at mine as I change into them, a tiny pair of pink shorts with green Tyrannosaurus Rex designs all over them. The top matches in the same shade of pink, two larger dinosaurs front and center, trying to touch each other's hands. Across the top of the dinosaur's heads, the shirt reads *High Five*.

Immy giggles at me, motioning for me to twirl around. I give her a little show, still unsure of how one person can make me feel so utterly complete.

"I picked this set because it's like the best of my bright and silly wardrobe with the best of your graphic tees and comfortable style."

"I love it," I tell her. And I mean it. I love the pajamas, but even more, I love how she brings out the best in me, no matter the circumstance. I love how she helps me to be brave, pushes me to succeed, and truly never sees an obstacle as impossible.

Under the clear night sky, we cuddle together in the slightly cool, late-night breeze. As we talk, we gaze at the stars and sip on champagne, the bubbles going to my head after my second glass.

I confess that while I have never considered therapy for my past issues, I think I'm ready to begin looking for a counselor I can trust. An unbiased observer who can help me further sift through the often-confusing feelings I have at war within myself.

Imogen feeds me chocolate-covered strawberries while we talk, holding them to my lips and laughing when I lightly nip them. She runs her fingers through my hair and over my neck before raking them over my sides and under the hem of my shirt.

"I'm so in love with you," she tells me. "It's always been you," she says as she climbs on top of me in a sudden but not unwelcome shift of our evening.

Her hips rock over my center, and I can already feel her heat radiating through the layers of our fabric. She pulls my shirt over my head, exposing my chest to the chilly breeze before leaning down to take one pert nipple between her teeth. She licks and sucks before moving to my other breast, repeating the process. Shimmying my shorts down around my hips, they quickly join my abandoned shirt on the ground.

Hands tease me relentlessly. Fingers trace circles on my skin before Imogen's lips join the party. Imogen licks against my skin, sliding herself down my body to settle between my legs. Parting my thighs, she doesn't tease any longer, bringing her tongue to taste me with long strokes of her tongue.

My head moves back and forth, taking in the sight of her moving between my legs while giving an equal turn to the stars above. And while the stars in the sky are insurmountable, I know my love for Immy is still larger than all the stars in the galaxy combined.

She licks and sucks at my clit, two fingers sliding deep into my heat, working me from the inside. Propping myself up at my forearms, I give over to the urge to give her my full attention, holding her eyes with mine as she pushes me closer and closer to the edge of oblivion.

It's an edge I willfully tip over, giving my body over to the pleasure she brings me. My thighs clench around her head, her name spilling from my lips over and over again.

Before the tremors fully leave my body, Immy somehow has me dressed, holding me tightly against her chest under a pile of blankets. When I move to reciprocate, she simply holds me closer, nuzzling into my neck.

I'm dazed and sated in her arms, in the very place I always want to be.

And just when I think it can't get any better, she reaches behind the pillows keeping us propped up and pulls out her matching quilt. Spreading it across us as we drift off to sleep together, it keeps us warm under the late-summer stars with the symphony of the seas creating the perfect backdrop to the most wonderful night of my life.

Thirty-Nine
Imogen

As late September morphs into early November, both Esme and I begin to pack our apartments. After our offer with the Farleys became official, we started to make plans for the move. And while I'm excited to begin this next stage of my life alongside the woman I love, it's bittersweet to be leaving my apartment.

I pull a few more books from my bookshelf, adding them to a rolling suitcase. It's just one of the many packing tips I learned on Pinterest while searching for ways to make my move as easy as possible. While the Farleys' house—*our* house—is only a few miles away from my current place, I dread unpacking and have been doing my damndest to make it go off without a hitch.

Thankfully, most of my furniture is staying behind, some of the small amount I have in savings going toward new furnishings Esme and I have picked out together.

My front door opening gives me pause as Esme calls out into the small foyer of my apartment, "I brought more boxes and packing tape!"

She brings the items into the living room, crouching down to where I sit on the floor to give me a kiss on the top of my head.

"Hi, sweetheart. I missed you," she says.

Sometimes, when she tells me that she missed me, I'm not sure if she means in the present or the past, but either way, I return the sentiment every time.

"How was your appointment?" I ask as Esme settles herself

on the couch where she begins to assemble boxes, expertly ripping pieces of tape in the exact length needed to slap over the edges of the cardboard.

Just a few weeks ago, Esme started therapy with a woman who came highly recommended by Campbell, of all people. While initially a rough start, she has fallen into a routine and now enjoys her twice-weekly sessions with Dr. Starr.

Flipping the box she finished taping, she grabs another flattened box and begins to repeat the process. "Really good, actually. We talked a lot about my mom today, about how I felt when she showed up at Luna Sea Lunacy, and the validity of those feelings. I think I'm slowly opening up to the idea of speaking with her. I don't think I'm ready to see her face to face, but maybe I can at least hear her out over the phone."

For her sake, if she decides to make that decision, I hope that whatever she learns from her mom helps to further put her at ease instead of pushing her back into being the broken woman she felt she was when she returned to Luna Harbor.

Not to say that I wouldn't be there for her if that did happen. If I've learned anything over the last ten months, it's that Esme Galloway and I belong together, that we're better when operating as a pair instead of as individuals. Then again, I think that I've always known that deep down inside. It just took her return for me to see it was an actual possibility.

We talk more about the progress she has made over the last few weeks and about what she hopes to overcome in the future, all the while filling boxes as if it's the most natural thing in the world.

Carrying boxes downstairs a short time later, we each fill our cars as much as we can and start on our way to our new home. One of the perks of knowing the previous owners of the house we just bought is being able to move things into the house before our official move-in date, and while we didn't officially get the keys to the house until yesterday, nearly all of our belongings are already there, piled in boxes in various empty rooms of our house...our *home*.

I laugh like a maniac as Esme pulls up next to me at a stoplight, *Dancing Queen* blasting from her speakers at full-volume. With her car windows down, she does a little dance in her seat, singing along to the lyrics at the top of her lungs before pulling in front of me when the light turns green.

Following her to our home, I'm surprised to see a few familiar cars when we pull into the drive, the sound of Esme's stereo finally quieting in the background. Swear to God, I could sing along the entire way to the new house with how loud it was coming from her car, and I didn't miss the few odd looks that were thrown her way as we made our drive through Luna Harbor.

Stepping out of the car, I pull the two rolling suitcases full of books from my trunk, while Esme hefts a duffle bag full of my clothes over her shoulder. She's lucky, only having to move most of her things a few yards from the garage apartment to the main house. Then again, that also opened her up to helping me more, so I really can't complain.

Pushing through the front door, I'm left speechless as our friends and family stand in the living room. IKEA furniture we had purchased and stored in the garage is fully assembled, and piles of gifts sit atop the coffee table.

"What the hell?!" Oaken calls out. "Who was supposed to be keeping watch for them?"

Several of our friends look around just as a rumpled Sunday walks back into the room. A few moments later, an equally disheveled Campbell follows the same path, reaching for a beer that sits on the counter separating the living room from the kitchen.

"Please tell me you two didn't just have sex in my house before I even had a chance to?" I ask the pair who vehemently deny any wrongdoings.

"We were just setting up a few things in the kitchen," Campbell says.

At the same time, Sunday speaks through a deep blush that spreads across her cheeks like wildfire. "I thought there was a leak in the bathroom and wanted a second pair of eyes to make sure nothing was wrong with your new house."

I can't help but laugh at the two of them. While they've been sneaking around for months now, they're oblivious to everything else happening around them—including the fact that we all already know they are hooking up.

Pizza arrives, and we scarf down slices before wiping greasy hands on too-thin napkins. Not wanting to mess up anything in our new home, our friends all wash their hands before helping to bring in the rest of the boxes from mine and Esme's car.

Birdie and Watson stroll through the door hand-in-hand, and even my parents stop by to see the house, oohing and ahhing as they take in the rooms and view from the small back patio.

We laugh as we so often do when together, Sunday begging us to stop at one point, saying if she laughed any harder, she would surely pee her pants.

Already, the space feels like it was built with us in mind, the perfect home to include all our found family that is constantly shifting and growing. Perhaps one day, we'll even share our small, sandy atoll with them, but for now, that is a secret of our new home we'll keep to ourselves.

As the night winds down, our friends leave one by one until it's just my parents, Birdie and Watson, and Esme and myself.

We share tight hugs with each of them as they get ready to leave, and I see my dad whispering something in Esme's ear that makes her smile as she pulls away from him.

My body hurts from the move, lugging boxes down from my second-story apartment, into cars, across our small town, and into their new space. I'm sweaty despite the fact that it's fall—stupid Florida heat—and all I really want to do is climb into the shower before sliding on my pajamas and crawling into bed with Esme next to me.

Instead of heading for the stairs like I had hoped, Esme plops onto our new couch, stretching her arms far above her head before patting the spot next to her. Above our heads, I hear movement but push it out of my mind as Esme reaches for the first gift on the table and holds it out to me.

One by one, we open the presents left behind by our generous family and friends, finding everything from fluffy, new towels to glasses, silverware, and dish towels. I take the kitchenware into the kitchen, setting it on top of the small, four-seater table we purchased for the space.

Moving to pull open the fridge for a bottle of water, I'm surprised to see that the entire space is already full with a collection of fresh fruits and vegetables. Juice containers line the top shelf while brand new condiments sit neatly on the built-in shelf on the door. I walk to the pantry, carefully opening the door just enough to peek inside. Again, instead of being met with an empty space, I find shelf after shelf of food—pasta and snacks, canned goods and dried beans. Absolutely everything we could ever need to start our life is already here.

Oil and vinegar?

Check.

Yogurt in a variety of flavors?

Check.

Croutons, pitted black olives, and those little crunchy onion things people put on top of their salads to make them a little less bland?

Check, check, and you guessed it...check.

"Hey, Es?" I call out across the house. "Can you come in here for a sec?"

She enters the kitchen with a smile on her face that slightly falls when she takes in my confusion. "Everything okay, sweetheart?"

At a loss for words, I open the pantry and gesture inside before walking back to the refrigerator where I repeat the process. "Did you already do grocery shopping?"

From the look on her face, Esme is just as confused as I am.

It takes a few minutes of searching, but we find a small card tucked in the top row of the refrigerator, right between a bottle of orange juice and a bowl filled with fresh lemons and limes.

Pulling it from the fridge, Esme slides her finger beneath the seal and pulls the card from its envelope. I read the shaky script over her shoulder before we turn to look at each other.

To Esme and Imogen,

For years, we feared leaving our beloved house behind, afraid that whoever owned it next would not love it as much as we have over the last five decades. It's a place where our own love story started, where we brought our daughters home to grow, and celebrated the birth of our grandchildren.

Now, with the house in your capable and loving hands, we can continue on to the next chapter of our lives while knowing that the legacy of our love lives on through you.

Enjoy your new home and the memories you will create in it together.

With love, all things are possible.

All the best,

Anita and John Farley

Together, we stand in silence, and I'm confident that Esme can feel the air in the house, already so filled with love as it wraps its arms around us both with blessings and hope for the future. As if it wasn't enough that the Farleys chose to sell us their former home at a steal of a price for the Luna Harbor market, they went through the trouble of fully stocking our kitchen, taking one of the stressful parts of moving off our plates.

"We've gotta send them a gift basket," I tell Esme after I can regain my composure.

She gives me a smile, pulling me into her arms. "I was

thinking we could carry on the tradition of using the Little Free Library that's at the foot of the driveway in their honor. Use it to honor the legacy they started in this home while helping others at the same time. But a gift basket could be cute, too."

I playfully push her away, groaning as I reach the foot of the stairs. "Let's go, sweet girl. It's time to shower, put some fresh sheets on the mattress, and go to sleep. We can build the bed tomorrow, but tonight, I need sleep."

Esme comes up the stairs behind me, holding onto my hips with her hands.

Before I can push the door to our new bedroom open, she pauses me and urges me to turn back toward her.

"Do you trust me?" she asks through a wry smile.

Quizzically, I look at the love of my life, though I don't pause to think about the answer. Because, of course, I trust Esme. The woman holds my heart in her hands, and I've never faltered in my decision to give it to her for safekeeping. "Of course, I trust you."

Leaning in, she places a kiss on my lips. It's sweet and chaste, reminiscent of some of the first kisses we shared.

"Close your eyes and keep them shut until I tell you to open them," she tells me softly. I obey her command instantly, plunging myself into darkness as my lashes flutter shut. With gentle fingers, she turns me around before reaching around my torso to open the door to our room. "No peeking," she tells me.

I hear the gentle squeak of the door as she pushes it open, but I don't dare open my eyes until she instructs me to do so. Instead, I allow her to take me by the hand, leading me into the center of our room.

When she has me where she wants, she presses another kiss to my lips, and I can't help but smile, my eyes still tightly squeezed shut. Then, standing behind me, she circles me safely in her arms.

"Welcome home, Immy."

Epilogue
Esme

Fifteen Years Later

ACROSS OUR BEDROOM, I HEAR THE SOUND OF IMOGEN'S HAIR dryer turning on. Familiar enough with her routine, I know that I have approximately twenty minutes until her hair is dry. Quickly, I get to work, putting my plan into motion.

Many things have changed over the past fifteen years, but as I knew it always would, my love for Imogen—for my Immy—has never changed. Actually, that might not be completely true because even after all this time, she still finds ways to make me fall deeper in love with her every single day.

We have lost friends and family over time, gaining others along the way. Grandma Birdie left us about three years ago, following in Watson's footsteps from a year earlier.

Oh, no, they didn't die or anything tragic like that, but they did decide to leave us for the greener pastures of traveling the world on a cruise. At ninety-two, Grandma Birdie has slowed significantly, but she often sends us pictures of herself and Watson seated around the dinner table with their much younger friends. It was hard for her to give up full control of The Grateful Thread to Imogen at first, but as she has become accustomed to life as a word traveler, she has yet to look back.

Working around our room, I light candle after candle as efficiently as possible. I have a lighter in each hand, clumsily flicking the one in my left hand while seamlessly using the second in my right. Taylor Swift—the cat, not the person—sleeps soundly at the base of our bed, the old man now old enough to drink legally in the United States. And yeah, you heard correctly. Turns out, Taylor Swift is a boy. Apparently, the little shit had been patrolling nearby neighborhoods for years, picking up all the single kitty females and growing quite the litter of kittens in his wake. Not wanting to contribute to the overwhelmingly large kitten population, we decided to remove the beast from his domain. Some days, nearly thirteen years after we brought him home, he still seems miffed about becoming an indoor cat, attacking plants and lizards that sneak into our now screened-in back patio. But most days, he's more than content to curl up at the foot of our bed, soaking up all the pets and treats he desires.

I run downstairs, grabbing a bottle of champagne we keep on hand for special occasions and a tray of chocolate covered strawberries—our favorite treat on extra special days.

Rushing back up the stairs and into our bedroom, I'm happy to hear the hair dryer is still in motion, the gentle sound of its hum only slightly muffled by the heavy, wooden door between us.

I place the bottle along with two crystal champagne flutes we used at our wedding on my nightstand, the strawberries sitting nearby on a tray atop our mattress. Smiling at our bed, I take in the quilt that covers the king-sized mattress.

It's the same one we used as children, only instead of the small, single-person quilts we each had, it's been sewn together to create one giant quilt suitable for our bed. New borders have been added, both to expand it in size and reinforce its strength, but still, it's the quilt that brought us together so many summers ago.

Staring at the pink and orange paisley panels, I smile as a

deluge of memories plays across my mind. Our first kiss and the first time we gently explored each other's bodies with tentative touches. The times it served as my only comfort from the cold, and the strength it brought me every time I looked at it when I was still clumsily finding my way back home. Our night at the lifeguard tower the year I first returned to Luna Harbor, and the gentle way in which Grandma Birdie continued to mend it over the years, keeping it as close to pristine as possible.

The hair dryer shutting off pulls me from my memories, and I hastily grab my phone, opening Spotify to our playlist. It contains songs from our childhood, pop songs we've learned to love together over the years, ballads that reminded us of one another in the years we were apart, a few notable mentions by Taylor Swift—the person, not the cat—and of course, the song I plan to play for Imogen when she steps out of the bathroom.

Not a minute later, the door is opening, Imogen affixing an elegant, cascading earring into her ear. Opening her mouth to speak, she turns fully into the bedroom, catching the sight before her for the first time.

Close to two hundred candles are lit across every surface of our bedroom. I know this because I counted as I lit them, praying I had enough time to pull this off but not so much time that they would turn into melted piles of wax and likely burn the house down.

Catching on to the scene almost instantly, she smiles at me, slowly walking toward where I stand at the foot of our bed.

"This..." she says softly, "is exactly like the night you proposed."

She's right, of course, as she always is.

I had proposed to Imogen the night we moved into this home together, knowing I couldn't wait a second longer for her to have my ring on her finger. Enlisting the help of Grandma Birdie, Watson, and Imogen's parents, I kept her occupied with opening gifts from our surprise housewarming party while they snuck into our bedroom through a ladder pushed against the side of our house.

When I finally got the all–clear—a horn honking three times as it drove away—I led Imogen to our room, pushed open the door to reveal hundreds of candles, and dropped to one knee in the middle of our unpacked room.

Tonight, instead of her ratty clothes she spent the day moving in, she's dressed in a silk robe, her hair and makeup are in place, ready for the fifteenth-annual Luna Harbor LGBTQIA+ Prom that is being celebrated this evening.

While I'm always proud of Immy, proud of what she has accomplished as an individual, I'm equally as proud of what we have accomplished together, and this event is the perfect example of what we're able to do when we combine our forces.

Since the first year she planned the event, surprising me with a recreation of the dance that put distance and years between us, it's grown into an event that encompasses an entire weekend. Our friends from the plaza still participate, and we raise funds throughout the year, hosting silent auctions and donation drives, drag brunches and stage shows. Teens from across the state of Florida make their way to Luna Harbor, where they come to meet others who are like them. They take classes and attend panels with local business owners, and they connect with friends old and new. We help those who are going to college with scholarship opportunities and those who need to escape unsafe situations do so as safely as possible. They're celebrated and nurtured, each of them learning to love themselves under the careful guidance of those who have come before them. Of course, the culmination of the weekend is the prom, and just like the first year, it's a celebration of all things queer love and life.

While we decided not to have children of our own, focusing all our energy on Taylor Swift—again, the cat, not the person—

the kids we meet each and every year on prom weekend become a permanent part of our found family. Many of them go on to return to our area to volunteer for future events, we've attended several weddings that came from relationships started at our events, and every year, we get more and more holiday cards from our extended family that now reside around the world.

I pull Imogen into my arms, pressing my lips to hers despite her perfectly-placed lip liner that I know she'll complain about me messing up.

"We both love this night more than anything, but I know we get pulled in a million different directions and sometimes barely have time to see one another until it's over, so I wanted to spend a few minutes with you before we leave—just us."

We walk hand in hand to my nightstand, where I hand her a glass of champagne. She accepts it graciously, and after a toast to our success, to our love, we clink glasses together before enjoying the bubbles as they travel across our tongues.

I take my phone and set it on the nightstand, reaching my free hand out to Imogen. I stare into her green eyes, still as entranced with them now as I was then. And though there are a few more wrinkles around her eyes than were there fifteen years ago, a few more gray strands of hair that dance in the sunlight, she's just as stunning as the day I met her as a wide-eyed girl willing to share her desk with the new kid at school.

"Dance with me before we leave?" I ask.

Her smile is soft as she nods, wrapping her arms around me on instinct.

And as she stays flush against my chest, I bend down to tap play on the song I've been waiting to play for her before the lyrics fill the room a second later.

Imogen bursts into infectious laughter, swaying along between my arms to the too-fast-to-slow-dance-to music as we get lost in each other's eyes and the sounds of our anthem.

You are the dancing queen

Young and sweet
Only seventeen
Dancing queen
Feel the beat from the tambourine, oh yeah…

THE END

SPECIAL THANKS

Normally, I start out this section by thanking my wife, but for Sew Into You, I feel it is important to start by thanking ABBA for their slamming hit, *Dancing Queen*, and to thank our Lord and Savior, Taylor Swift, for giving me endless hours of company while writing Imogen and Esme's story.

Laura—my absolute rockstar of a wife—without you, none of my books would exist. I'm forever grateful to you for pushing me to do what I've always wanted, for your support, your beautiful brain that often helps me spot plot holes, your patience when I ask you to read the same chapter for the seventh time, and the love you shower me with each and every day.

Katie Warren—one of my first Bookstagram friends—you've been such a help since the beginning of my journey as an author. From posting about my very first book, to setting up book tours, and helping to find ARC readers for Sew Into You, you constantly go above and beyond and I'll never be able to fully put into words what it means.

Cady and Tori of Cruel Ink Editing & Design—the two beauties who are responsible for not only my gorgeous cover but stunning formatting as well—without the two of you, my books would be but a Word doc, forced to live its days on my computer where it would never see the light of day. Sure, I could trust my work in the hands of others, but why bother when I've already found the best in the two of you?

Tiffany—editor extraordinaire and the best cheerleader there is—you've grown to be much more than my editor over the last six books. When I say that I would not be as strong a writer as I am today without you in my corner, I absolutely mean it. Thank you for always reigning in my comma usage, helping me to come across as a writer who knows what I'm doing, and for always cracking me up with the hysterical notes you leave in the margins.

Last, but perhaps most importantly, a huge thank you to anyone who has ever been told that you are different. To our trans youth fighting against unfair legislation every day, our drag queens who have had their beloved storytimes taken away, and the authors who have had books unfairly banned. This one's for you, because not only do you inspire me each and every day, but you are the change I wish to see in the world every day.

OTHER WORKS

Broken Sparrow Collection:

Inked

Etched

Standalone Books:

The Arrangement

Beautiful Games

Knotty Valentine (Sapphic Novella)

ABOUT AMITY

Amity Malcom was born in Pennsylvania. She began writing short stories while still in elementary school-including a total page turner about how her mother loved to fish. Her mother does not love to fish and is actually terrified by ocean creatures.

She now resides in Florida with her wife, two completely insane but lovable cats and one neurotic but adorable dog.

When not writing steamy characters and happily ever afters, Amity can be found watching professional soccer, exploring Florida's many theme parks, and campaigning for LGBTQIA+ rights.

AMITY'S SOCIAL MEDIA

Instagram: AmityMalcomWrites

Facebook Page: AmityMalcomWrites

Facebook Reader Group: amitymalcomsmavens